Enjoy all of these American Girl Mysteries:

THE SILENT STRANGER A *Kaya* Mystery

PERIL AT KING'S CREEK A *Felicity* Mystery

TRAITOR IN WILLIAMSBURG A *Felicity* Mystery

SECRETS IN THE HILLS A *Josefina* Mystery

THE RUNAWAY FRIEND A *Kirsten* Mystery

SHADOWS ON SOCIETY HILL An *Addy* Mystery

THE CURSE OF RAVENSCOURT A *Samantha* Mystery

THE STOLEN SAPPHIRE A *Samantha* Mystery

DANGER AT THE ZOO A *Kit* Mystery

MIDNIGHT IN LONESOME HOLLOW A *Kit* Mystery

A THIEF IN THE THEATER A *Kit* Mystery

A SPY ON THE HOME FRONT A *Molly* Mystery

THE LIGHT IN THE CELLAR A *Molly* Mystery

— A *Kirsten* MYSTERY —

THE RUNAWAY FRIEND

by Kathleen Ernst

Published by American Girl Publishing, Inc.

Questions or comments? Call 1-800-845-0005, visit our Web site at **americangirl.com**, or write to Customer Service, American Girl, 8400 Fairway Place, Middleton, WI 53562-0497.

Printed in China
08 09 10 11 12 13 LEO 10 9 8 7 6 5 4 3 2

PICTURE CREDITS
The following individuals and organizations have generously given permission to reprint illustrations contained in "Looking Back": pp. 170–171—wheat field, © Stuart Westmorland/Corbis; girl with cattle, © North Wind/North Wind Picture Archives; pp. 172–173—Dala painting, American Swedish Institute; cabin, Wisconsin Historical Society, Old World Wisconsin Outdoor Museum; oxen, © Carl and Ann Purcell/Corbis; woman with scythe, Minnesota Historical Society; mittens, courtesy of Judith Lary; pp. 174–175—girl milking, Wisconsin Historical Society; quilting bee, State Historical Society of North Dakota; wolf, © John Conrad/Corbis; pp. 176–177–Ojibwa mother and child, Minnesota Historical Society; Fredrika Bremer, © Krays, Johansen/Archive Iconographico, SA/Corbis; Swedish keepsakes: contents courtesy of Anna Hamilton, keepsakes chest courtesy of Barbara Johnson Antiques, Rockford, IL; Swedish festival, © Raymond Gehman/Corbis.

Illustrations by Jean-Paul Tibbles

Cataloging-in-Publication Data
available from the Library of Congress.

For the Writer Chicks—
*with thanks for **everything***

Table of Contents

1 A Guest from Sweden 1

2 The Sheriff's Visit 21

3 Lost Heart 29

4 To the Shanty 39

5 Another Missing Treasure 53

6 The Newspaper 66

7 A Strange Delivery 84

8 Surprise in the Root Cellar 97

9 Anna Provides a Clue 115

10 Looking for Answers 129

11 The Wolf 146

12 Choices 160

Looking Back 171

Glossary of Swedish Words 179

1
A Guest from Sweden

"Oh Lisbeth, isn't the wheat beautiful?" Kirsten exclaimed. She and her cousin were carrying both news of visitors and buckets of water to the fields. Papa and Uncle Olav had started cutting wheat just that morning, and the uncut grain rippled like a golden ocean beneath the breeze. Clouds scudded across the August sky. Kirsten, her two brothers, and her parents had been in Minnesota for only a few weeks, but mornings like this made her glad they had dared to take the long journey from Sweden.

Lisbeth put down her heavy buckets, giving her hands a rest. "Papa worked extra hard last spring to get so much land plowed and planted. Thank goodness he was able to buy Starke and Fläckis to pull the plow. Papa kept saying"—Lisbeth lowered her voice to imitate her father—"'We must plant enough grain this year to take care of *two* families.' He was lucky to have Erik's help, too." Erik Sandahl was a neighbor.

"It's too bad we couldn't get here sooner," Kirsten said. "This morning, *my* papa said, 'Lars, we must work extra hard to get all the grain safely into the barn. My brother did the spring plowing and planting for both families. Now we must do our share and more.'"

"Well, they're certainly working hard!" Lisbeth said, pointing. In the far field, Uncle Olav and Papa were swinging big scythes with practiced ease. Each man used the sharp, curved blade to cut a swath of wheat stalks and sweep the stalks aside in a neat row. In the closest field, where the oat crop had already been cut, stacked, and left to dry, Erik Sandahl and Kirsten's older brother, Lars, used pitchforks to toss dry bundles into a wagon. Starke and Fläckis, Uncle Olav's prized team of oxen, were hitched to the wagon. Other than switching their tails at pesky flies, the oxen stood patiently.

The girls took up their buckets and carried them on toward Lars and Erik. "We have company!" Lisbeth called as they approached.

"Who's come?" Erik pulled a kerchief from his pocket and blotted sweat from his face before accepting a dipper of water. He was a year or two older than Lars. Although he was growing his first beard and carried a man's responsibilities, Kirsten already thought of him as a friend.

"Reverend Trulsson, all the way from Saint Paul," Lisbeth told them. "He's brought a writer from Sweden! Miss Mobeck isn't going to settle here, but she's visiting immigrants so she can write a book that will help other Swedish people decide whether they want to come."

"Our visitors brought newspapers and mail from Maryville," Kirsten added, excitement bubbling inside. "Lars, there was a letter from Mormor!" Kirsten couldn't wait to hear what her grandmother had written. Mama had pressed the letter against her cheek, then set it aside to be opened later. Only a quiet moment, with just the family gathered, would be right for sharing such a precious letter.

"What's this about a letter?" Papa asked. He and Uncle Olav had cut through the stubble to join them.

Lisbeth told the men about their guests. "I expect they'll spend the night," Uncle Olav said.

"Oh, yes!" Lisbeth agreed. "And Mama said to ask if you could spare Lars and Erik to go tell our neighbors."

Kirsten's papa squinted at the sky, frowning. "I don't know that we can spare the boys. Clouds are building. A storm could blow up anytime, and we've got acres of wheat left to cut. And what we *have* cut needs to be bundled and stacked and—"

"Yes, yes." Uncle Olav clapped an arm around his brother's shoulders. "There is plenty of work to do. But we must be good hosts as well. I think we can spare the boys."

Papa still wasn't sure. As the two men discussed the situation, Kirsten set her buckets in front of Starke and Fläckis. She patted Starke's sweat-dark flank fondly while he slurped. After the oxen had hauled the grain into the barn, Uncle Olav and Papa would spread sheaves on the barn floor and lead the oxen over them until the tiny kernels of oats or wheat had been separated from the stalks. Once the kernels were cleaned and sacked, the oxen would haul the heavy load to market. "Drink up," Kirsten told the oxen. "You deserve it."

When the buckets were empty, Kirsten turned back to the others and noticed Erik examining a puffy blister on his right hand. "Erik!" she said. "You need gloves!"

"Gloves cost money," Erik said. "But don't worry, my hand is fine." He made a flicking motion with his thumb and gave her a sly grin. "I can still beat you at marbles."

"Do you have them along?" Kirsten asked eagerly. "Maybe we can play tonight!"

He shook his head. "*Nej.* They're back at the

shanty. But I promise, we'll play again soon."

On his journey from Sweden, Erik had carried three marbles in his pocket. The small spheres had been made of clay, colored in rich tones of blue, green, and rose, and baked hard. "The last Christmas my father was alive, he gave them to me," he'd once told Kirsten. "They're all I have to remember him by."

Now, Papa and Uncle Olav had made their decision. "Lars, you can go fetch the Berg brothers," Uncle Olav said. "Do you know the way?"

Lars nodded. "I remember from the day we took Starke and Fläckis over." Uncle Olav was the first man in the area to purchase oxen, and he sometimes rented or loaned the team to other farmers.

"Good," Uncle Olav said. "And Erik, are you willing to go tell the Greens and the Vanstrums?"

Erik grinned. "Of course!"

Lisbeth squeezed Kirsten's hand, looking delighted. "We're going to have *more* company!"

❤

A little later, Kirsten sprinkled sand on a section of the floor of her family's cabin, wet a brush in a bucket of water, and began to scrub. Kirsten's younger brother, Peter, and Lisbeth's younger sister, Anna, were helping Mama and Aunt Inger in the big house across the yard. Most of the guests coming to the Larson farm that evening would probably spend the night, and Mama and Aunt Inger were both making ready to open their homes. Mama wanted the old cabin's plank floor scrubbed smooth and white.

"Lisbeth," Kirsten said, "tell me about the people who are coming to visit."

Lisbeth, who had come to the cabin to keep Kirsten company, gave the coffee grinder another crank. "The Vanstrums have a little girl. The Berg brothers are bachelors, and everyone calls them Big Berg and Little Berg. You've met all of them before."

Kirsten tried to attach faces to those names.

"I must have met a thousand new people since leaving Sweden," she said. "On the boat across the Atlantic Ocean, and on the train to Chicago, and on the riverboat to Minnesota. And once we got here to the farm, we've had company as often as not!"

"You don't mind, do you?" Lisbeth asked. "Here in America, everyone opens their homes for travelers."

"Oh no, I don't mind," Kirsten said quickly. Although the steady stream of strangers was sometimes overwhelming, she didn't want Lisbeth to think she was selfish! Kirsten knew that her family was lucky to have a stout little cabin of their own already. Most newly arrived immigrants weren't so fortunate, but Papa's brother, Uncle Olav, had left Sweden when Kirsten was only three years old. He'd found good land in Minnesota. He'd also married Inger, a widow with two daughters. Kirsten's cousins had lived in the cabin until recently, when Uncle Olav had built the big new house for his family. Uncle Olav, Aunt Inger, and

Lisbeth and Anna had made Kirsten's family feel welcome in many ways.

"I don't think you've met the Greens yet," Lisbeth added. "Johanna Green is really nice. Her father has a temper, though. Ooh!" Lisbeth leaned back against the wall. "My arm's getting tired. Want to switch? I'll finish the floor if you'll finish grinding the *kaffe* beans."

Kirsten traded places with her cousin. She was getting used to cranking the grinder, for the Larson farm was far enough from a gristmill that the women usually had to grind their own corn. Kirsten set to cranking, enjoying the rhythmic *scriitch* of Lisbeth's scouring and the sharp scent of crushed coffee beans.

"I'm glad Aunt Inger is making *kaffe* tonight," she said. "Mama and Papa have both seemed anxious lately. It will be a treat for them."

"Everyone's worried about getting the wheat safely into the barn," Lisbeth said. "A hailstorm, or even a heavy rain, could ruin the crop."

Kirsten sighed. For months, her family had focused on just one goal: making the long journey to their new home safely. Sometimes it seemed as if they hadn't had any time to enjoy that accomplishment before a whole new round of worries set in.

Well, they were working as hard as they could. "Tonight," Kirsten declared, "let's help everyone forget their worries!"

❤

By the time whippoorwills began calling through the twilight, the Berg brothers, the Vanstrums, and the Greens had arrived. Johanna Green was tall for her age, and thin, with eyes that seemed older than a ten-year-old's should. She greeted Kirsten shyly.

Kirsten gestured at the basket Johanna held. "What did you bring?" she asked.

"Some turnips from our garden."

"Oh, good—the turnips here are so sweet!" Kirsten said, and was pleased to see Johanna smile.

"We have a horse," Johanna whispered.

"He loves turnips, too. He lets me ride him. Would you like to come meet him sometime?"

"That would be fun!" Kirsten said. "If I can. I have a lot of chores."

"Me too." Johanna nodded knowingly.

The men built smoky smudge fires in the yard to help keep mosquitoes away and then carried the kitchen table and benches outside. The women spread out bowls and platters, and everyone loaded plates with catfish and venison, rye bread and sweet butter, turnips and carrots and peas.

Miss Mobeck, the guest of honor, was a friendly young woman with a heart-shaped face, intelligent eyes, and brown hair looped over her ears. Her pretty wine-colored dress and the softness of her hands made Kirsten guess that Miss Mobeck had never done farm work. The author greeted each family warmly, though, taking a moment to repeat names as if she wanted to remember every one. "Green is not a familiar name," she said, pausing by Johanna's parents. "Yet you are Swedish?"

"My Swedish name is Sjögren," Mr. Green replied. "It's a hard name for Yankees to say. Now that we're here, it's important to become American."

"Ah." Miss Mobeck nodded.

Kirsten, who was passing among her new neighbors with a plate of pastries, had to listen carefully to the conversation. The guests came from different parts of Sweden and pronounced certain words in ways that sounded strange to her ears. When she stopped in front of the author, she asked clearly, "Would you like a fruit tart?"

"Tack!" Miss Mobeck exclaimed. Kirsten smiled, understanding that easily: *Thank you!*

"It's Kirsten, isn't it?" Miss Mobeck tipped her head thoughtfully. "Many Swedish children will immigrate in the next few years. So tell me, Kirsten. What's been the hardest thing about settling into your new home?"

Kirsten paused. "The wolves," she said after a moment. "I can hear them howling at night." She shuddered.

"That must be frightening!" Miss Mobeck said. Then she looked around the circle. "Are they a danger here?"

"We do often see wolves skulking around," Uncle Olav said. "You can usually scare them away if they come too close, though. And it's unlikely that a wolf would attack a person. There's too much wild game in the woods for them to eat."

That reminder made Kirsten feel a little better.

The author took a bite of her pastry. "Mmm! These tarts—what fruit are they made with?"

"They're called 'cranberries,'" Kirsten told her, struggling with both the English word and a stab of homesickness. Back in Sweden, Kirsten had gone every year with her grandmother to the deep forest to pick their favorite fruit, lingonberries. Those tiny red berries would soon be ripe, but Mormor would have to pick them by herself now.

"There's plenty of food in Minnesota,"

Mr. Vanstrum was saying. "Although new settlers should be warned that the first few years will be hard. Sugar, salt, *kaffe*—those things are luxuries."

"Do you see Indians often?" Miss Mobeck asked. "Everyone in Sweden is very curious about them."

"Our cabin is close to an old trail, and sometimes Indians stop by," Mr. Green said. "They usually just want some food. Tell your readers to be prepared for that."

What will it be like to see Indian people? Kirsten wondered. Life in Minnesota was so different from life in Sweden!

Miss Mobeck leaned forward eagerly. "What other advice do you have for Swedes considering moving to America?"

The men glanced at each other, considering such an important question. "Don't go into debt," Mr. Vanstrum said finally. "It's hard to repay even a small debt."

"That's good advice," added Big Berg. Kirsten thought his nickname suited him well.

Both of the Berg men were big, but Big Berg was an inch or so taller than his younger brother.

"That's why most of us are still making do with grub hoes," Little Berg explained. "One day we'll buy our own team of oxen, but we don't have enough money yet."

"A good team of oxen is the most important purchase an immigrant can make," Uncle Olav added. "I was only able to buy my team last spring. With the oxen, and with Erik's help, I was able to plant twice as much grain this year."

Miss Mobeck was scribbling in a little notebook. "Erik, are you a hired hand here?"

"Nej," he said. "I settled on my own land last spring, about two miles from here. I have to live on my claim, and cultivate at least some of the land within a year. Otherwise, someone can take it away from me." He gave a good-natured shrug, and the firelight glinted off his red-gold curls. "I built a shanty, and I'm growing some corn, but it's pretty lean there.

I often work here in trade for these ladies' fine cooking."

"So you immigrated alone?" Miss Mobeck asked. "Some of the men in Sweden are trying to decide if it is better to come alone or to come with a family."

Erik looked away for a moment. "It's true I have no real family here in the Maryville district," he said finally. "But I've never felt lonely."

"Erik often stays here with us," Aunt Inger explained. "And sometimes the men go to his place and work together."

"It's important for Swedes who have been here for a few years to help newcomers," Uncle Olav said simply. "It is no easy thing to come to this country and start over."

"Hardest on the women," Mrs. Green murmured. Then she looked startled, as if surprised to realize she had spoken aloud. "But we must carry on, of course."

Kirsten glanced at Mama. She sat on a bench a little apart from the others. A ball of wool yarn was in her pocket, and despite the fading light, she was knitting. Kirsten sighed. Even now, Mama couldn't stop working.

Papa spoke up for the first time. "With hard work and God's help, I believe a poor family can succeed here." He nodded at Miss Mobeck. "Tell your readers that. Many of us left the old country because we wanted our children to have a better life. As long as we don't lose heart, I believe that will happen."

He smiled at Kirsten, and she suddenly felt warm and safe inside. "We won't lose heart, Papa," she promised.

Miss Mobeck put one hand on her chest. "It does *my* heart good to see this 'New Sweden' in the wilderness," she said. "Now, let's enjoy this fine evening!"

With that, everyone set aside serious topics. Miss Mobeck read aloud a story by Hans Christian Andersen that she'd brought. Lisbeth and Anna sang a Swedish hymn. Then all the men joined together in one of the old national songs. "Up, Swedes! For King and Fatherland," they sang, their deep voices ringing across the clearing and into the woods beyond.

A shiver rippled over Kirsten's skin as she watched her father sing. She desperately wanted Papa to be proud of her! Despite what she'd told him, though, she did sometimes worry about losing heart. She missed her grandparents, and she grieved for her friend Marta, who had died on the trip to Minnesota. The trunks holding some of the Larsons' most precious possessions—including Kirsten's doll, Sari—had been left in storage because her family had run out of money and had walked the last leg of the journey. And there had been little but hard work and worry since arriving. As Kirsten watched the men sing together, she hoped that her family *would* succeed in making a good new home here in America.

Then Little Berg brought out his fiddle. He didn't play very well, but no one minded. His brother held out his arm to Miss Mobeck, and soon they were leading an energetic polka across the grass. Kirsten was glad to see Mama put her knitting aside for a dance with Papa. Mrs. Vanstrum had adorned her faded dress with a rosette made from blue ribbon, which fluttered cheerfully as she and her husband danced. The Greens stood to one side, watching. But everyone else seemed ready for a frolic.

When Little Berg began his next tune, Erik presented himself to Kirsten with a formal bow. "Miss Larson? Will you do me the honor?" He guided her in a fast, whirling waltz. Kirsten was breathless by the end of the dance. "This is the most fun I've had since coming to Minnesota!" she gasped.

Erik laughed. "We must always spare some time for fun." Then he went off to ask Anna to dance.

Little Berg didn't pack away his fiddle until long after dark. "Everyone is welcome to spend the night here, of course," Uncle Olav announced. "It will be safer to travel home in the morning."

"I'm going to take my family home tonight," Mr. Green said.

Aunt Inger's forehead wrinkled. "Are you sure? We've got plenty of room."

"We need to get home!" Mr. Green said, so forcefully that some of the other guests turned their heads. Lisbeth nudged Kirsten to say, *See what I mean about Mr. Green's temper?*

Kirsten looked quickly at Johanna, who stood near her parents, staring at the ground. Kirsten didn't like to see her new friend heading off into the dark night. Why wouldn't her father let them stay with the Larsons, where it was safe?

2
The Sheriff's Visit

Mr. Green drew a deep breath and lowered his voice. "*Tack*. But we really must go. I have my musket and a lantern. We'll be fine."

"I'll walk with you," Erik offered. Then he looked at Papa and Uncle Olav. "I'll spend the night at my own place, but I'll be back before the dew dries tomorrow morning so we can get back to the harvest."

After the Greens and Erik left, Aunt Inger and Mama spread quilts and blankets on the floors of the big house and the little cabin. With careful planning, everyone had a place to sleep. Kirsten squeezed into a bed in the cabin with Anna and the Vanstrums' two-year-old daughter. The little girl kicked in her sleep, and once the last candle was blown out, someone sleeping on the floor began to snore loudly—but listening to snores was better than listening to wolves howl! With the echoes of Swedish songs and dance tunes in her head, Kirsten soon drifted to sleep.

Everyone was up before dawn, and after a breakfast of bacon, fried eggs, potatoes, and more coffee, the Vanstrums and the Berg brothers headed for home. Miss Mobeck carried her carpetbag out to the wagon where Reverend Trulsson was waiting. "I enjoyed your hospitality," she told the Larsons. *"Tack."*

"Remember us to Sweden," Mama said softly.

"Will you be coming back this way?" Kirsten asked Miss Mobeck. "Maybe you could stop here again!"

The writer beamed. "I would love to! After I travel farther west, I'll circle back here and see how you all are doing."

Everyone waved as Reverend Trulsson drove Miss Mobeck away. Then Papa said, "Well, we've got a full day of work waiting.

Let's be at it. Erik will be here any moment."

Just then Kirsten heard something unexpected: hoofbeats. "Someone's coming!" she exclaimed. Horses were rare here. Had one of the Greens returned?

The rider who emerged from the trees was a stranger, though, on a sand-colored horse. He wore dark trousers, and a dark wool vest over a white shirt now stained with sweat and dust. A silver badge glinted in the morning sunlight. Kirsten stepped closer to Mama.

The man reined up hard in front of the group and said something in English. Kirsten recognized the words "Olav Larson."

Uncle Olav frowned. "*Ja?*"

The man said something else. Kirsten watched Uncle Olav's expression fade from wariness to dismay. He began to argue with the man.

"What's this?" Papa asked. "Olav, what's happening?"

The stranger pulled a piece of paper from his coat pocket. He held it out to Uncle Olav, pointing at something written near the bottom. Uncle Olav's shoulders sagged.

Alarm was twisting knots in Kirsten's stomach, and she tugged at Lisbeth's sleeve. "What are they saying?" she hissed.

Lisbeth's gray eyes were wide. "It's the sheriff! He's come to take Starke and Fläckis away!"

Kirsten couldn't believe Lisbeth had understood correctly. "Take Starke and Fläckis away? *Why?*"

"It has something to do with Erik!" Lisbeth squeezed Kirsten's hand.

Kirsten felt more bewildered than ever. What did Erik have to do with the sheriff wanting their oxen?

Lars looked alarmed. "We need the oxen to harvest and clean our grain!"

Uncle Olav protested again, waving his arms at the fields, and Kirsten was sure he was making that same point to the sheriff. The sheriff looked unhappy, but he shook his head, tapping the paper one more time before folding it away.

Finally Uncle Olav jerked his head toward the barn. The sheriff kneed his horse and trotted in that direction.

"Olav, what's *happening?*" Papa demanded.

"There must be some mistake." Uncle Olav ran a hand over his hair. "Last spring, Erik needed money to get started on his own place. He'd been working here on the farm for me, and I knew he was trustworthy. I didn't have any cash to loan him, and the bankers in Saint Paul wouldn't loan him money because he owned nothing of value. So I signed the loan paper with him. The bank wouldn't have given him the loan otherwise."

"I knew nothing of this loan," Papa said. His tone held a note of accusation. Kirsten edged even closer to Mama. She had never heard Papa cross with his brother before, and she hated that as much as she hated what the sheriff was doing.

"It took place before your family arrived," Uncle Olav said. "I saw no need to discuss it. Erik is a Swede, a hardworking young man who needed a little help to get started. If people hadn't helped me when I first arrived in America, I would not have been able to accomplish everything you see here."

"But Erik hasn't repaid the loan to the bank," Papa guessed grimly. "And now the sheriff is taking the oxen to satisfy the debt. Do I understand this correctly?"

"Ja," Uncle Olav admitted. "The sheriff said the team will be sold so that the bank can get its money back. But—but this *must* be a mistake! Erik has been cutting wood on his land to earn the money he needs to make the payment."

"Why didn't the sheriff go talk to Erik?" Lars demanded. "He'd be able to explain everything."

"The sheriff said he arrived at the shanty at dawn," Uncle Olav said. "Erik wasn't there."

The sheriff rode out of the barn leading Starke and Fläckis. Kirsten felt tears sting her eyes as she watched the oxen lumbering behind the sheriff's horse. Anna started to sniffle.

The sheriff paused by the group and said something in a low tone to Uncle Olav. "He said that he's sorry he has to do this," Lisbeth murmured. "And that he'll try to wait a couple of days before selling the team."

Then the sheriff rode away, with Starke and Fläckis plodding along behind.

"This must be a mistake," Uncle Olav said again, breaking the silence. He turned to Papa. "We need to find Erik, so he can explain what happened. Perhaps we can still get the oxen back."

Papa's face had settled into hard lines. "If a storm comes before we get the grain in . . ." He let his voice trail away.

"Let's go," Uncle Olav said. "Lars, you and Peter start on chores."

Aunt Inger, who had been listening with her arms folded across her chest, spoke up. "Perhaps Erik decided to spend the night with the Greens."

"We'll check there on our way," Papa said.

"Erik will be able to explain everything, Papa," Kirsten called. "I know he will!"

Papa raised a hand, showing her that he'd heard. But he didn't smile.

3
Lost Heart

The men returned two hours later, their faces still grim, and everyone gathered at the big house to hear the news.

"We went first to the Greens' cabin," Papa reported. "They invited Erik to sleep there last night, but he said no. The last they saw of Erik, he was walking on toward his place."

"All alone?" Kirsten burst out. Something terrible might have happened in those dark woods!

"We walked the trail carefully," Papa said. "There was no indication of any trouble."

Uncle Olav sank onto a bench and put his elbows on his knees. "And when we got to Erik's shanty," he said, "there was no sign of him."

Aunt Inger poured two steaming cups of coffee. "Did it look as if he had left for good?" she asked quietly, handing a cup to her husband.

"His hoe and his frying pan were still in the shanty," Uncle Olav said. "But if Erik left in a hurry and wanted to travel light, he might have left those things behind."

"What are we going to do now?" Mama asked. Her voice was tight. "Is there any way we can scrape up enough money to buy the oxen back ourselves?"

"Not until we get the grain cut, and dried, and cleaned, and off to market." Uncle Olav spread his hands. "And without the oxen . . ."

He didn't need to finish his sentence. Without the oxen, the family faced an overwhelming job.

"I'm afraid Erik realized that he wouldn't be able to repay his debt," Papa said, "and decided to move on before the law caught up to him."

"Surely he wouldn't have done that!" Kirsten protested.

"Reverend Trulsson delivered two newspapers along with your letter," Aunt Inger said. "He just put them aside, knowing that people would take what was theirs. If Erik was one of the subscribers, maybe he realized by looking at the date on the newspaper that his time for repaying the loan was up."

"But Erik would have talked with you about that!" Kirsten insisted.

"Kirsten, hush," Papa said. "These are matters you don't understand."

"Yes, Papa," Kirsten whispered. She knew better than to argue with her father, but she couldn't believe that Erik would have run away from a debt, leaving the Larsons to suffer the consequences. Why, just yesterday he'd promised her another game of marbles . . .

Kirsten caught her breath. "Papa, did you notice if Erik's marbles were in his shanty? He keeps them in a little cloth bag, hanging from a peg."

Papa's frown deepened. "We were hardly looking for toys when we were at the shanty!

We have much more serious things to worry about than your games!"

Kirsten struggled to keep her face from showing how Papa's words had stung. She had been trying to point out something that might be helpful. If Erik had left for good, he would have taken the marbles with him. If they were still at the shanty, that surely meant that he was planning to come back! But she didn't dare try to explain that to Papa now.

Mama spoke into the silence. "Let's read my mother's letter," she said. "That will cheer us up."

Kirsten had almost forgotten the letter from Mormor. Now she watched as Mama fetched the letter, broke the sealing wax, slid a piece of paper from the envelope, and began to read:

My dearest daughter,

I hope this finds you all well. I have little news, but Mr. Pehrson is traveling and was kind enough to say he'd carry a letter as far as the coast, so I took pen in hand. We are doing as well as can be expected, although our hearts are heavy with knowing how far away you are. As I write this, you have been gone for only two weeks and are still at sea, but the time does go by slowly.

Please write soon and tell us all about your new home. What flowers grow in Minnesota? Were you able to buy a cookstove for a reasonable price? Your father is anxious to hear about the farm. What livestock do you have? What crops are you raising? He wonders about these things every day.

Give our love to everyone.

Mama was blinking by the time she finished. Kirsten could tell that she was trying not to cry. Kirsten was, too. It was lovely to hear from Mormor! But the letter made Kirsten miss her grandmother more than ever.

Papa shoved himself to his feet. "We have to get to the field," he said gruffly. "Lars, we need you and Peter as well."

"And there's work to be done in the garden,"

Mama said, dabbing her eyes with her apron. "Run along, girls."

"I'll be right there, Mama," Kirsten promised. "I want to stop at our cabin first." Mama nodded.

Before Kirsten had left Sweden, Mormor had given her a little amber heart. Kirsten usually wore it on a ribbon around her neck, and she loved to rub the smooth surface when she was feeling homesick. Yesterday she'd taken the necklace off during chores and left it hanging from a peg that Papa had driven into the wall over her bed. Now, with so many things going wrong, she wanted the reassurance of feeling the amber heart hanging around her neck.

Kirsten hurried to the cabin, plunged through the door—and came to an abrupt halt. The peg over her bed was empty.

"But—it was—it *must* be here!" Kirsten stammered. Perhaps the ribbon had somehow been knocked from its peg. She pulled back the blankets on the bed, searching carefully. Then she dropped to her knees and hunted under the bed, checking behind the legs and in the crevice along the wall.

Nothing.

A tear spilled over and rolled down Kirsten's cheek. What could have happened to her precious amber heart? *I never should have taken it off,* she thought. She was tempted to run to her parents, but she quickly discarded that idea. Papa was angry about the oxen. Mama was homesick. Now was not the time to tell either of her parents about losing her gift.

Instead she wiped her eyes and went to join her cousins. Lisbeth and Anna were in the garden, picking beetles from the potato plants. Kirsten had already come to dislike this particular chore, but if it was not done, the insects would destroy the plants.

Lisbeth gave her a sorrowful look. "Isn't this terrible? I've never seen everyone so upset."

"It *is* terrible!" Anna cried. "It was horrible for that mean man to take our oxen!"

"The sheriff was just doing his job." Lisbeth sighed. "It's really Erik's fault."

"I still think it's a misunderstanding," Kirsten protested. "Erik would never run off and leave a debt for your father to pay!"

"Probably not," Lisbeth said slowly. But she didn't sound sure.

I need to visit Erik's shanty, Kirsten thought. *If I find his marbles there, then perhaps the rest of the family will believe that he hasn't run off for good.* She wasn't sure how she could get away from her own chores long enough to make the trip to the shanty, but she was determined to try.

Right now, though, she had a new problem. "I need to ask you both about something else," she said. "I left my amber heart hanging on the peg above my bed yesterday, and now I can't find it."

"Oh, no!" Anna wailed.

"I'm sure it will turn up." Kirsten tried to sound confident. "And I don't want to mention it to Mama. But I was wondering if either of you noticed it yesterday."

Anna shook her head, wide-eyed. "I don't remember seeing it at all."

"I saw it there yesterday afternoon when we were cleaning," Lisbeth said. She pinched a beetle from the underside of a leaf and dropped it into a bucket. "It *may* have been there when we went to bed, but with the shadows—I just don't know."

Anna lowered her voice. "Do you think someone stole it?"

"Nej!" Kirsten said quickly. She hadn't meant to imply that at all! Although . . . lots of people had been in and out of the little cabin yesterday evening. Any one of their guests might have seen the amber heart hanging on the wall.

Lisbeth and Anna exchanged a troubled glance. "That heart was beautiful," Lisbeth said soberly. "If someone was desperate for money, it might have been tempting. Perhaps Erik . . ."

Kirsten didn't want to even *think* about what Lisbeth was suggesting. She wished she'd never told her cousins about losing the necklace.

Kirsten also wished that she hadn't urged

Miss Mobeck to come back to the Larson farm. It was embarrassing to think that the writer might learn about the sheriff seizing the Larsons' oxen. What if she wrote about it in her book? What would her readers think? Would Kirsten's grandparents read about it and worry even more?

I can't let that happen, Kirsten thought. She couldn't imagine where Erik had gone. But maybe she could find some answers in his shanty.

4
To the Shanty

As Kirsten picked potato bugs and hoed rutabagas, she found herself looking over her shoulder, hoping to see Erik emerging from the woods with a grin and a good explanation for the confusion. "It's all a mistake!" she imagined him saying. "I'll get enough money from the lumber I've cut to pay off my loan. I'll go straighten things out with the sheriff." But the hours passed with no sign of Erik.

No one had much to say that evening when the two families gathered after dinner at the big house. Uncle Olav read aloud from the Bible, but his voice was heavy. Kirsten stared at Aunt Inger's favorite Swedish rug without seeing the pattern. It was hard to feel hopeful when everyone was so unhappy. When Uncle Olav was finished, Kirsten's family said good night and went home to bed.

The next morning, Kirsten waited for a quiet moment to talk with her mother. When the two went outside after breakfast to fetch water, Kirsten said, "Mama, I think it's important to see if Erik's marbles are still at the shanty."

Mama regarded her. "Kirsten," she began. "Your papa told you—"

"Papa thinks I'm worried about games, but I'm not!" Kirsten protested. "If the marbles that Erik's father gave him are still there, then Erik must be coming back. It would tell us that he didn't mean to run away and leave Uncle Olav with the debt."

"Finding the marbles wouldn't tell us anything for sure." Mama stopped, put down her bucket, and placed her hands on Kirsten's shoulders. "I don't want to hear any more about this. We all need to help Papa and Olav get the crops in. There's no time for anyone to go back to Erik's shanty."

"Yes, Mama," Kirsten said in a small voice. She wouldn't say any more about it. But she wouldn't forget, either.

That day everyone worked in the field. Papa and Uncle Olav brought in the stacks of oats that had already dried, piling them onto small sleds that were usually used to haul rocks from the field and dragging the heavy loads to the barn. It hurt Kirsten's heart to see the men doing the oxen's work.

Mama and Aunt Inger cut wheat. They were not strong enough to swing the heavy scythes, but they could make slow progress with small hand sickles. Kirsten's job was to tie the cut grain into bundles, using several stalks twisted together as twine. Lars and Lisbeth collected the new bundles and piled them into shocks to dry. Peter and Anna helped by carrying water and the stones that the men used to sharpen the sickles.

Yesterday's lovely breeze had danced away, and by the time the sun stood high in the sky, Kirsten's dress was soaked with sweat. Her sunbonnet hung limply around her face. Her back ached. Mosquitoes whined in her ears. No matter how hard she tried, she couldn't make her bundles of wheat as tight and even as Papa or Lars could. *I wish we'd never come to America!* Kirsten thought miserably. Life had been hard in Sweden, too, but no sheriff had ever come to the Larsons' door to make everything worse.

When Peter and Anna brought lunch to the field, Kirsten sat where she was, too tired to move. Anna handed each person an open-faced sandwich, or *smörgås,* of buttered bread and cheese. "Papa," Anna said hesitantly when she reached her father. "I think Kulla is gone."

Uncle Olav groaned. "That cow," he muttered. "We don't have time for her tricks today!"

Kirsten often helped with milking, so she knew the cows well. Kulla was mischievous. She'd kicked the milk bucket over more than once, and she sometimes knocked over a fence rail or two and wandered off.

"I can go look for Kulla," Kirsten volunteered. Today, the idea of wandering into the unknown woods didn't seem any worse than the prospect of spending the afternoon in the wheat field.

Uncle Olav and Papa exchanged a glance, considering. "That may be best," Papa said. "Lars and Lisbeth are more help to us here, and Anna and Peter are a little too young to send off."

"Is it safe for Kirsten to go?" Mama asked. She looked as wilted as her sunbonnet.

"There's plenty of daylight left," Uncle Olav said.

"And Kulla leaves a clear trail," Lisbeth added. "She usually heads toward the creek."

"If you don't find the cow by mid-afternoon, turn around and come home," Mama told Kirsten.

"And keep a sharp lookout for landmarks along the way," Papa added. "We have no time to come looking for a lost girl."

Was that the only thing that worried Papa—

that if she got lost, he'd have to waste time coming to find her? Kirsten got up and brushed her hands on her skirt, avoiding his gaze.

"Yes, Papa," she said. "I'll be careful not to get lost."

❤

The cow's trail through tall grass and brush was easy to follow. It soon led into the woods. The Minnesota forest looked different, and smelled different, from the Swedish forest near Kirsten's old home. Even the birdsongs were unfamiliar. Soon, though, Kirsten decided she was glad that Kulla had gone wandering. The air was cooler beneath the trees. After Kirsten snapped off a bushy elm branch to wave about her head, the mosquitoes and biting flies left her alone. *I just won't think about wolves,* Kirsten told herself. Still, she picked up a few stones to carry, ready in case she needed to drive some wild animal away.

Kulla's meandering trail led to the creek,

just as Lisbeth had predicted. But when Kirsten reached the creek, there was still no sign of the cow. Kirsten took a careful look around. Had she missed something? There—a low branch had recently been broken, and hoofprints in the damp ground showed that Kulla had headed upstream. The cow had wandered farther than Kirsten had expected, but at least traveling along the creek would keep them both from getting lost.

Some time later, Kirsten finally caught up with the errant cow. "Kulla!" she scolded. The cow, who stood munching some particularly thick grass growing along the creek bed, looked over her shoulder. Her expression seemed to say, *Oh? Were you looking for me?* Kirsten felt exasperated, but it was hard not to smile, too.

Now that she had found the cow, Kirsten allowed herself a few moments of rest. She'd put part of her lunch into her pocket, and she sat on the sun-dappled creek bank and munched the last of her bread and cheese.

As she took a better look around, she sat up straighter. That mossy boulder looked familiar. So did the big tree leaning over the water. Kirsten realized that she had been here once before, after an afternoon she'd spent grubbing weeds from Erik's garden while Lars and Erik hoed his corn. They'd traveled on the road that day, not through the woods. But before they'd headed home, Erik had brought them to the creek to splash and cool off.

"We're not too far from Erik's shanty!" Kirsten told Kulla. "Come along, cow! You've come this far, you can walk a little farther."

Kirsten had brought a length of rope with her. After knotting it loosely around Kulla's neck, she led the way upstream. Before too long she spotted the well-worn path that led to Erik's land. A few minutes later, Kirsten and Kulla emerged from the trees.

Erik had built his shanty against the side of a hill. Packed earth formed the back wall, and upright poles the other three. A small door marked the opening of the little root cellar that he'd dug into the hillside. Corn plants grew on the acre or two of land he'd been able to clear so far. Stacks of logs, cut to lengths about as long as Kirsten was tall, stood high beside the shanty.

Kirsten couldn't see any sign of life on the little farm. *Could Erik have run away and left all this?* she wondered. The farm might not look like much yet, but it represented many hours of backbreaking work.

"Erik!" Kirsten shouted. "Erik, are you here?" No answer. She tied Kulla to a sapling and approached the shanty. "Erik?" Kirsten waited for another moment. Then she pulled the latchstring and let herself inside.

The windowless shanty was dim, and Kirsten left the door open. She looked first for the little pouch of marbles. There it was, hanging in its place of honor! She blew out a long, relieved breath, certain now that Erik had not run away for good.

But if Erik hadn't run out on the loan, where *was* he?

Kirsten scanned the small room. As far as she could tell, everything was in place. The mattress stuffed with marsh hay, and the single blanket that covered it, were tidy on the narrow bed frame built against one wall. What little cooking Erik did took place on a flat stone in one corner, and his frying pan was tipped upside down nearby so that it wouldn't rust. The heavy hoe he used to turn soil and root out weeds stood in one corner, next to his pitchfork.

"Erik, where did you go?" Kirsten whispered. She went back outside with a heavy heart.

The turnips, beets, and potatoes in Erik's garden were drooping in the sun, so Kirsten hauled water from the creek and watered the vegetables. Then she stepped back into the shanty and paused, looking again at the pouch of marbles. It was sad to see it hanging here in this now-lonely place.

Kirsten plucked the pouch from the wall and poured the marbles slowly into her hand.

She hadn't had any real toys of her own to play with since coming to Minnesota. It had been so much fun to play marbles with Erik! He would place one of the marbles in the center of a circle drawn in the dirt. Then they'd take turns flicking marbles, trying to knock the center one from the circle.

Kirsten knelt and placed the green marble on the floor. Then she positioned the rose-colored marble, which had always been her favorite, on her forefinger. Squinting, she took careful aim and flicked the rose marble at its target. The two marbles connected with a satisfying little *click.*

Then the green marble rolled away along the seam between two floorboards . . . and disappeared.

Kirsten could hardly believe her eyes. She scrambled to the spot where the marble had vanished. "Oh, no!" she moaned. What had looked in the dim light like a knot in one of the floor planks was actually a knot*hole,* just big enough for a marble to fall through.

Kirsten's cheeks burned. If Erik ever came back—no, *when* Erik came back—how would she explain herself?

Maybe she could get the marble out. She poked one finger into the hole and wiggled it frantically. No luck. She couldn't feel anything.

Then she sat back on her heels. She couldn't feel *anything?* That seemed strange.

Kirsten frowned at the hole for a moment before getting up and fetching the pitchfork from the corner. She tipped the fork so that one sharp tine slid into the knothole. Then she lifted the fork. The entire board popped easily from the floor.

Holding her breath, Kirsten pushed the loose board aside and knelt beside the new opening. Erik had dug out a narrow space beneath this part of the floor. She spotted the marble right away and snatched it up triumphantly.

Once the marble was safely back in its pouch, Kirsten looked back into the hidey-hole. What else was hidden there?

The first thing she pulled out was a folded newspaper. The paper looked fresh, not yellowed and brittle—it was probably one of the newspapers Reverend Trulsson had brought. One corner of a page had been torn away. "What was here?" Kirsten asked the silent shanty as she fingered the ragged edge of paper. She looked into the hole again, hoping that the torn section might be there, but the hidden space was now empty.

No, wait. It wasn't. A piece of dark canvas blended into the dirt so well that Kirsten had almost missed it.

She reached down, and her fingers closed around something hard, wrapped in the cloth. When she pulled it out and unfolded the cloth, she found a small rectangular case made of a hard black material. A tiny gold latch held it closed. Kirsten slid open the latch with one thumbnail, leaned toward the light spilling through the doorway, and opened the case.

The case held a photograph, captured on glass, of a young woman. She stared serenely at the camera, her hands folded on her lap. She wore a simple dark dress with no adornments.

Kirsten stared at the photograph. The young woman was lovely. But who was she?

5
ANOTHER MISSING TREASURE

"You found a *photograph?*" Lisbeth sounded disbelieving. She and Kirsten were doing the milking that evening.

"Shh!" Kirsten looked over her shoulder, but the cows were their only company in the stable. "I shouldn't have looked at Erik's private things. So please don't tell anyone!"

"I won't," Lisbeth promised. "But why would Erik hide something like that?"

"I don't—Kulla, stop it!" Kirsten pressed a hand to her cheek, which was stinging from the swipe Kulla had just given it with her tail.

"Tie her tail to her leg," Peter advised. "What did Erik hide?"

Kirsten almost fell off the milking stool. She hadn't heard her little brother enter the stable!

"The . . . um . . . well, he hid the reason he went away," she said quickly. "Shouldn't you be fetching water?"

"Nej."

"Well, run along anyway," Kirsten said firmly. She waited until Peter disappeared, then rolled her eyes at Lisbeth. "Brothers!" Once the cow's tail had been temporarily secured, Kirsten settled back on the low stool. "Anyway, I can't figure out why Erik would hide a photograph."

Lisbeth thought that over. The only sounds in the barn were a rhythmic *zing-zing* as streams of milk hit the girls' pails, and the contented munch of the cows chewing their cuds. Kirsten usually liked this time of day. Today, though, her mind was tumbling with too many questions to savor the peace.

"The photograph must be of a sweetheart, don't you think?" Lisbeth asked finally.

"Why wouldn't Erik want us to know that he has a sweetheart?"

"I don't know," Lisbeth admitted.

"At least the photograph makes me think even more that he isn't gone for good," Kirsten said. "He wouldn't abandon a picture of his sweetheart!"

"Maybe the girl in the photograph *used* to be his sweetheart," Lisbeth suggested. "Maybe she broke his heart, and he wants nothing more to do with her! Maybe Erik decided to make a whole new start in life and left everything behind that reminded him of the past."

Kirsten considered, doubtful. "I suppose that could be it."

"I know you liked Erik," Lisbeth said sympathetically. "We all did! But I've been in Minnesota long enough to know that sometimes people move on. It's hard to get a farm started, and some people . . . well, some give up. If Erik realized he couldn't pay his debt, he may have headed farther west, thinking the law couldn't catch up with him."

"Don't you think he would have said goodbye?"

"Not if he didn't have the money to repay

the loan," Lisbeth said. "What could he have said to Papa?"

"Erik just didn't seem like the kind of person to do something like that," Kirsten said. She felt hurt and angry and sad, all jumbled together.

"That's true, but he was hiding more than one secret from us. The photograph you found proves that. And why did he spend money on a newspaper subscription when he was in debt?"

Kirsten sighed. "I don't know. It wasn't fair to Uncle Olav."

"We didn't know Erik as well as we thought we did, and now he's probably gone for good," Lisbeth said. "The best thing we can do is stop fretting about him." She carried her bucket toward the door. "Are you about done with Kulla? Let's get this milk strained so we can help with supper."

Kirsten concentrated on her milking. *Squeeze, pull. Squeeze, pull.* If only life in America were so simple.

❤

That night Kirsten lay awake long after dark, thinking over what Lisbeth had said. Lisbeth had accepted Erik's disappearance. *But I can't,* Kirsten thought. She wanted to find Erik, and to hear the truth from him.

Then an eerie howl outside made her bones go cold. *Wolves.* They sounded very close tonight.

Kirsten crept from bed and tiptoed to the window. She saw the dark silhouette of a wolf padding past the house . . . and another . . . and another. A pack of wolves was circling her cabin! One stopped, threw its head back, and let loose another howl. The others joined in. Their chorus seemed to hold all the fear and loneliness in the world.

Kirsten shut her eyes and put her fingers in her ears. "Go away," she whispered. *"Go away!"*

Then she jumped as someone squeezed her shoulder. "Don't be afraid, Kirsten," Papa murmured. "You're safe inside, and the cows are safe in the stable."

He guided her back to bed with a gentle hand on her arm. Kirsten felt the calluses on his palm, and a rough scab at the base of his thumb where something had torn the skin. As she slid beneath her sheet she felt an ache inside, half sweet and half sad. Papa's reassurance did make her feel better, but she wished he hadn't seen how much the wolves frightened her. Now more than ever, he needed her to have a stout heart.

Kirsten finally dozed off, but some time later she woke again. She opened her eyes and saw Mama sitting at the table. Mama had poured grease into a dish and added a wick made from a rag. She was leaning close to the feeble light, and the faint *click click click* of her knitting needles whispered in the silence.

Oh, Mama, Kirsten thought. Was Mama so worried about the coming winter that she felt she needed to knit even after an exhausting day doing field work? Or was she so worried about the loss of the oxen—and everything that meant for the Larsons—that she simply couldn't sleep?

Her parents were doing everything they could to take care of the family. As Kirsten lay watching her mother, remembering the feel of her father's work-roughened hand, she tried to think how she could be more helpful . . . and *that* turned her thoughts back to Erik. If he couldn't repay his loan, the least he could do was continue to work on the farm until the grain was safely harvested!

But Erik could be far away by now. How could she ever know? Searching the shanty had turned up some interesting finds, but nothing useful . . .

No, wait. Erik had tucked away the newspaper only *after* tearing off the corner of one page. That corner must have contained something important—something he needed to take with him.

Reverend Trulsson had delivered two newspapers. The Larsons didn't subscribe to the newspaper. If one copy had been Erik's, the other copy must belong to the Greens, the Vanstrums, or the Berg brothers. If Kirsten could find that second copy, she could discover what story had been printed on the corner Erik had torn away. Perhaps *that* might tell Papa and Uncle Olav where to look for Erik.

❤

"Aunt Inger," Kirsten said the next morning as she delivered the morning's milk to the cool root cellar, "Reverend Trulsson brought two newspapers from Maryville. If one was for Erik, do you know who the other one was for?"

Aunt Inger shook her head. *"Nej,"* she said, "I don't." She gave Kirsten a curious look as she began pouring the milk into shallow pans, where it would sit until the cream separated and rose to the top. "The newspapers were written in English, Kirsten. You wouldn't be able to read them. Why do you ask?"

Kirsten scrambled to think of a reasonable answer. "Well, I—I was thinking it might be good if I could learn a little English before school starts in the fall." She felt her cheeks flame and hoped Aunt Inger didn't notice. After all, she *was* dreading the start of school. "I was going to ask Lisbeth to help me."

"I'm sure Lisbeth would be glad to help you." Aunt Inger laid pieces of cloth over the pans to keep flies out, then wiped her hands on her apron. "But not this morning, I'm afraid. We've got field work waiting!"

❤

Kirsten trudged through the morning, struggling again to tie the new-cut grain into neat bundles. Mama's eyes were smudged with fatigue. Papa's face had settled back into hard lines. Everyone was worried about getting the grain safely harvested, and no one had gotten enough sleep.

Just when Kirsten had started hoping that Kulla might break through a fence again, a woman's shouted greeting rang through the morning. *"God morgon!"* Mrs. Vanstrum stood at the edge of the field, waving.

Aunt Inger waved back. "Olav," she called. "I need to go greet our guest."

Uncle Olav nodded. "Yes, of course."

Mama straightened, rubbing her back. Papa squinted up at the sky, then stared over the acres of wheat that still needed cutting. *Say something, Papa!* Kirsten urged him silently. She could see how badly Mama needed a rest.

Finally Papa nodded. "We'd all be glad if you'd fix a lunch to bring us," he told his wife. "You run along as well, Kirsten. Help with the food." Kirsten went gratefully.

Mrs. Vanstrum waited at the edge of the field. A basket dangled from one arm. She also had a ball of yarn in her apron pocket, and a warm, thick sock was growing from the knitting needles that danced in her hands. She cocked her head toward the fields as the Larson women approached. "Where are the oxen?"

Aunt Inger sighed. "Come inside, and we'll tell you."

In the kitchen, Kirsten sliced bread and cheese as Aunt Inger told the story.

"That's a loss for all of us," Mrs. Vanstrum said sadly. She looked at Mama. "And a harsh welcome to your new home."

"We're trying to stay hopeful," Mama said. "But it's hard. Olav planted extra grain because we were coming—and now we could lose everything!"

Mrs. Vanstrum handed her basket to Mama. "Perhaps this will lift your spirits. I know that you don't have sheep yet, and I have more wool than I need. I'd be glad if you could make use of this."

"Oh!" Mama's eyes glowed as she lifted fat skeins of yarn—cream-colored, black, and gray—from the basket. "I was almost out of yarn."

Kirsten wanted to hug Mrs. Vanstrum.

"How can I thank you?" Mama murmured, fingering the yarn.

"No thanks needed." Mrs. Vanstrum smiled. "That's what neighbors do."

"Well, it was kind of you to walk over with it," Mama said.

"Actually, I had another reason for coming." Mrs. Vanstrum's smile disappeared. "When I was here the other night, I lost a rosette made from a blue ribbon. Did you happen to find it?"

Kirsten went very still, remembering the sweet silk flower Mrs. Vanstrum had worn on her dress. Mama and Aunt Inger exchanged puzzled looks. "No, we didn't," Aunt Inger said.

"It was a little thing, but all I had that was pretty," Mrs. Vanstrum said. "My husband gave me that ribbon when we were courting. Well, perhaps it will turn up." She stood. "I need to get back home."

Kirsten caught Mrs. Vanstrum's eye. "I'm sorry about your rosette," she said. "I'll keep watch for it."

"Thank you, dear," Mrs. Vanstrum said. "That's all I can ask."

Kirsten took a deep breath. It was hard to question an adult she didn't know well, even someone as nice as Mrs. Vanstrum. "And if you don't mind me asking—do you and your husband subscribe to the newspaper?"

"Nej." Mrs. Vanstrum shook her head. "Even if one of us could read English, that's a luxury we can't afford."

Aunt Inger sent Mrs. Vanstrum on her way with the last of the cranberry tarts tucked into her basket. Kirsten watched as their neighbor started on her long walk home, knitting as she went. *Well,* Kirsten thought, *I've learned two things already.* The second newspaper Reverend Trulsson had delivered must belong either to the Berg brothers or to the Greens.

The other bit of information was disturbing. Surely it couldn't be coincidence that Mrs. Vanstrum's ribbon rosette and her own amber heart had disappeared on the same night!

6
The Newspaper

As Kirsten finished helping the women pack lunch baskets, someone else called, *"God morgon!"* Johanna Green stood in the doorway.

"Come inside!" Kirsten said happily. Johanna gave her a small smile but didn't meet her eye.

"Is something wrong?" Aunt Inger asked. "Is your mama sick?"

"Nej." Johanna looked embarrassed. "We let our fire go out. I came to fetch some coals, if I may."

Kirsten tipped her head, startled. People back in Sweden sometimes lost their fires, but usually it happened first thing in the morning, if their banked coals had gone cold overnight.

It was a little odd that Johanna had come to borrow coals in the middle of the day.

Aunt Inger was too polite to show surprise. "Of course you may!" She used a piece of kindling to scrape several chunks of half-burned wood, still glowing orange beneath a thin blanket of ash, from the stove's firebox into a small iron frying pan. "Those coals won't last long. You'll have to run home!"

"I will," Johanna said gratefully. "And I'll come right back and return the skillet."

"Kirsten, why don't you go with Johanna?" Aunt Inger suggested. "You can bring the skillet back and save her the extra trip."

Kirsten grinned. "I'd like that!" Then she remembered Papa, and the wheat, and the worries. "But . . . shouldn't I go back to the field?"

Aunt Inger and Mama exchanged a glance and seemed to come to a quick, silent agreement. "You can come back to the field work when you get home," Mama said.

"Now, go!" Aunt Inger made a shooing

gesture with her hands. "Go quickly, or the coals will die and you'll have to try again!"

❤

When the panting girls arrived at the Green clearing, they found Johanna's mother waiting on the cabin's front step, twisting a handkerchief in her hands. "Thank God you're back," she said. She squeezed her daughter in a hug, then put one arm around Kirsten's shoulders as well. "And you came, too! That was kind, Kirsten. I hate to have Johanna traveling alone through the woods. Anything could have happened!"

"But it didn't, Mama." Johanna squirmed free. "Let me get these coals inside."

"I was glad to come," Kirsten said. She stopped in the doorway, still struggling to catch her breath. Then she noticed that the entire floor was damp. A bucket and scrub brush sat in the middle of the room. "I'll wait here, so I don't track dirt onto your clean floor."

"Nej." Mrs. Green beckoned Kirsten inside. "Come in, dear. It was so silly of us to let the fire go cold."

Johanna slid the coals into the stove's firebox, added some shavings, blew gently across the wood, and smiled as new flames wriggled to life. "There," she said triumphantly.

"Thank goodness it isn't winter," Kirsten said. "We wouldn't have been able to run in deep snow!"

Mrs. Green shuddered. "I don't even want to think about the winter."

"You've made your cabin a pretty place to spend a winter," Kirsten said as she took her first good look around. Johanna's home was not much bigger than her own family's cabin. It had two glass windows, however, and both a front door and a back door. Those additions made the interior much lighter. Mrs. Green had cut scallops along strips of brown grocery wrapping paper and had tacked them to her shelves. Houseplants in crocks twined around strings up the sides of the windows.

"I try to do what I can." Mrs. Green's smile seemed a little sad. "It's hard to make a nice home here in the wilderness, though."

"What a beautiful *tine!*" Kirsten exclaimed, stepping closer to a shelf so that she could examine the delicately carved trinket box.

"My grandfather made it for me, back in Sweden," Johanna told her. "See where he carved my initials into the design?" She pushed the *tine* away from the edge of the shelf, as if worried that her precious box might fall.

Kirsten felt another pang of homesickness. Most of the mementos her family had brought from the old country were still stored in trunks miles away. *Except for my amber heart,* she thought, and maybe that was gone for good. Straightening her shoulders against the sadness, Kirsten tried to distract herself. "What's that?" she asked, pointing at a splash of brilliant blue on the shelf.

Johanna picked up a stack of papers and handed them to Kirsten. "These are sugar wrappers. Haven't you ever seen one before?"

When Kirsten shook her head, Johanna explained, "Sugar here comes in a hard cone. Mama and I save the wrappers. They make a nice dye for yarn."

Kirsten touched one of the wrappers. She'd never seen such a deep, rich blue. If only *her* family could afford to buy sugar from a store! Uncle Olav and Aunt Inger collected honey and boiled maple sap into syrup, so the Larsons didn't want for sweets. But as Johanna put the papers back on the shelf, Kirsten's heart ached with a bit of pure envy. Mama would take such joy in coloring some of her knitting yarn with this lovely blue!

"Johanna, don't leave the papers out in plain sight," Mrs. Green said. "They might get stolen."

That word snatched Kirsten's attention. "Stolen?" she asked. "Has something been stolen from you?"

"No," Johanna said. "Mama just worries." She quickly tucked the blue wrappers away beneath a dish towel. "Kirsten, do you have time to meet someone before you go?"

Kirsten considered telling Johanna about her amber heart, but then decided against it. "*Ja,*" she replied, following her friend back outside. "Who do you want me to meet?"

"Our horse! But we need to stop at the garden first."

As Kirsten helped dig several small turnips from the ground, she couldn't help noticing that the garden wasn't nearly as well maintained as the house. Weeds had straggled into the rows of vegetables. A pile of newly dug carrots waited to be carried inside. Beyond the garden, Mr. Green's small wheat field needed harvesting, too. His corn grew among stumps that needed to be wrestled from the stubborn soil.

Kirsten forgot all that, though, when she met the Greens' horse. "Oh, he's beautiful!" she cried. Even in the stable's shadows, the horse's coat gleamed a glossy black.

"And he's gentle and smart," Johanna said, patting the horse's neck. "His name is Svarten." She showed Kirsten how to offer a turnip on her palm.

Kirsten laughed as she felt Svarten's hot breath and soft nuzzle on her skin. He accepted the turnip at once. "He's friendlier than oxen," she exclaimed—then abruptly remembered that Uncle Olav's oxen were gone. "I surely do miss Starke and Fläckis, though."

"I'm sorry about what happened," Johanna said quietly. "Erik was always kind to us. Sometimes when my father had gone to the mill or to buy supplies, Erik stayed here so that Mama and I wouldn't be alone."

As the girls headed back to the cabin, Kirsten glanced again at the garden. She knew that she needed to get back home . . . but surely a few more moments wouldn't hurt. "It looks as if you dug carrots this morning," she said. "Can I help you get them out of the sun before I go?"

Johanna hesitated. "That would be nice," she said finally. "Papa's gone fishing today, and Mama doesn't do much outside. I have trouble keeping up with it all."

Mrs. Green didn't help with outside chores?

Kirsten pictured Aunt Inger, bustling with energy, and Mama, quieter but never shirking what needed doing. And they had three girls to help them! "I'm glad to," Kirsten assured her friend. "It won't take long."

The girls filled baskets with carrots, lugged them to the root cellar behind the cabin, and packed the vegetables away in sand-filled barrels. "There," Kirsten said. "You'll enjoy them all winter!"

"Tack," Johanna said gratefully.

As they turned to leave the cellar, Kirsten noticed something unusual. "Johanna," she exclaimed, "why did your father put a latch on the inside?" The cellar's stout wooden door had an outside latch, of course, for the door had to be shut tightly to keep cool air in and hungry bears and raccoons out. But this root cellar also had a latch on the *inside.*

Johanna pressed her lips together in a tight line and hurried into the sunshine. "No real reason." She slid the wooden bar on the outside latch firmly into place.

Kirsten's smile faded. She hadn't meant to hurt her friend's feelings!

They stopped back at the cabin so that Kirsten could fetch her aunt's frying pan. Mrs. Green had gone back to her scrubbing. Kirsten didn't want to interrupt, but she also didn't want to lose this unexpected opportunity. "Excuse me," she said hesitantly. "Reverend Trulsson brought a couple of newspapers when he came. Did one of them happen to be for you?"

Mrs. Green nodded. "Why, yes. Did you want to borrow it?"

"Yes, ma'am," Kirsten said eagerly.

Johanna looked puzzled. "Do you read English?"

"No, but I know I need to learn." *And that,* Kirsten thought, *is the truth.*

Mrs. Green found the newspaper in a trunk. "My husband reads English. He's already read this, though. You're welcome to keep it."

"Tack," Kirsten said. Now she might learn something useful about Erik!

Johanna's mother chewed her lower lip. "Are

you sure you need to go home right away? My husband will be back by early evening, and it would be safer if you waited until he could walk you home. Indians travel through sometimes, and rough men looking for work. And there are wolves in the forest, and bears, and—and all sorts of things!"

Kirsten *didn't* want to walk home alone, and she wished that Mrs. Green hadn't spoken her fears aloud. Still, Kirsten knew that her family expected her long before dusk. "I'll be fine," she said, trying to believe it. "Thank you anyway." After retrieving Aunt Inger's frying pan, Kirsten gave Johanna a special smile and started on her way.

"Come back soon, if you can," Johanna called after her.

Kirsten waved, thankful that her friend had forgiven her for asking about the latch. Kirsten puzzled over that latch, though, as she hurried toward home. Why would the Greens want to lock themselves inside a dark root cellar? It made no sense.

Something else seemed strange. Mrs. Green had been scrubbing the center of the floor, but the whole floor was already damp. Didn't she start in the far corner and work toward the door? And if she'd been working inside this morning, hadn't she noticed that her fire needed tending?

Well, Johanna's parents might have strange ways of doing things, but Kirsten was glad that the Greens' fire had gone cold. She'd tracked down the second newspaper! Maybe, once Lisbeth had read the section that matched the corner Erik had torn from *his* newspaper, they'd have a real clue about his disappearance. Kirsten tucked the paper more firmly under one arm and began to run.

❤

Kirsten didn't have a chance to show Lisbeth the newspaper until late afternoon, when Aunt Inger and Mama asked the two girls to start supper in the big house. "Lisbeth," Kirsten said urgently, "I need your help with something." She fetched the newspaper and spread it out on the table. "Is your English good enough to read this?"

Lisbeth leaned closer, then nodded. "Yes. But why . . . " Understanding washed over her face. "Does this have something to do with the newspaper you found in Erik's shanty? I thought you were going to stop fretting about Erik."

"I can't!" Kirsten said. "Not when he's caused so much trouble for our family. I hate seeing everyone so worried and angry." She gave Lisbeth a pleading look. "Please, Lisbeth? Will you help me?"

"Oh, all right," Lisbeth said. "But we have to be quick about it! If Mama finds us—"

"I'll start on the soup," Kirsten offered quickly. "You can read. It was the bottom corner of this page." She tapped the newspaper.

While Kirsten washed peas, Lisbeth studied the paper. "It's mostly advertisements," she reported. "'Pocket knives, stationery, fishing tackle . . .'" She read on, describing all kinds of merchandise the storekeepers in Saint Paul offered, until she reached the end of the page.

Kirsten put a kettle of water on the stove. "Erik wouldn't have run off to Saint Paul to buy a pocket knife or fishing tackle. What's on the other side?"

The newspaper rustled as Lisbeth turned the page. "Let's see . . . the corner on this side has notices." With one finger marking her place, she began to read aloud. "'The *Mary C.* reached our dock yesterday with a full freight for the merchants of Saint Paul.'"

"Not helpful," Kirsten said.

"'Sidewalks are now being laid near the Post Office, an improvement long needed.'"

Kirsten shook her head. *"Nej."*

Lisbeth slid her finger down to the next item. "'Notice: Whereas my wife, Sally Braxton, has without just cause left my home, I hereby forbid all persons from sheltering her or trusting her on my account.'"

After turning that one over in her head for

a moment, Kirsten shook her head again. "I can't imagine how that could have anything to do with Erik."

Lisbeth continued reading. "'Wanted: A man to build a fence around two village lots—'"

"Maybe that's it!" Kirsten cried. "Maybe Erik wanted to get that job!"

Lisbeth looked doubtful. "Why would Erik leave in the middle of the night and walk all the way to Saint Paul to get a temporary job?"

"Well..." Kirsten tried to make sense of her idea. "Maybe Erik was interested in that job because it *was* temporary. Maybe he thought he could go make some quick money and then come back."

"If so, then why didn't he tell anyone?" Lisbeth asked. "He could easily have let us or the Greens know about his plans. And it's a long way to Saint Paul. Don't you think he would have gotten a few hours of sleep and waited for daylight before heading out?"

Kirsten's flush of excitement drained away. Lisbeth was right. The job announcement didn't explain Erik's abrupt disappearance. "Is there anything else in that section?" she asked.

Lisbeth read to the end while Kirsten mixed a soft dough for dumplings. Neither girl could guess why any of the notices or advertisements might have prompted Erik to disappear. "I'm sorry, Kirsten," Lisbeth said. "It was a good idea."

"But it didn't help us." Kirsten sighed. *Maybe I should just leave things alone, as Lisbeth said,* she thought gloomily.

Lisbeth began picking over some berries, which would be served with fresh cream. "Did you find your amber heart?"

That question did nothing to cheer Kirsten up. "Not yet."

"And Mama told us that Mrs. Vanstrum's rosette is missing." Lisbeth's blue eyes were troubled. "I hate to say this, Kirsten, but your amber heart and Mrs. Vanstrum's pretty rosette would make two nice gifts for any lady. If that woman in Erik's photograph is his sweetheart, well . . ." She didn't finish.

Kirsten couldn't argue. It was certainly possible that Erik had seen the two trinkets on the night of the gathering and seized upon the opportunity to present a sweetheart with gifts. If the young woman had broken his heart, maybe he'd thought he could win her back with the presents. The very idea left a sour taste in Kirsten's mouth.

Then she remembered Mrs. Green's comment about the blue sugar wrappers. "Lisbeth, Johanna's mother was fretting about someone stealing some pretty paper they've been saving. But when I asked if they were missing something, Johanna said no."

"Mrs. Green is sweet, but she's a worrier," Lisbeth said flatly. "We've all gotten used to her fussing."

Kirsten began dropping spoonfuls of dough into the kettle, where the peas and some salt pork were simmering. "Why do you think the Greens walked home the night of the party, then? Don't you think she would have felt safer waiting until morning?"

Lisbeth turned her palms up. "Who knows?"

Kirsten sighed. Despite her best efforts, they didn't know anything more than they'd known that morning. She was hot and frustrated and tired.

Not as tired, though, as the others would be when they finally came in from their day in the field. Where were Starke and Fläckis right now? Had the sheriff already sold them, or was there still a chance the Larsons might get them back?

Kirsten squared her shoulders. She was not ready to give up searching for Erik—and some answers. "Thank you for helping with the newspaper," she told Lisbeth. "I'll just have to think of something new to try."

7
A Strange Delivery

The Larsons were just sitting down to supper when they heard an odd clinking sound outside. Kirsten and Lars exchanged puzzled glances, but Lisbeth and Anna grinned. "It sounds like Gustaf!" Anna cried.

"Bring him in," Aunt Inger said. "I'll set another place at the table."

Kirsten followed her cousin outside as an elderly man shuffled to the house. He wore cracked brogans, dusty trousers, and a patched jacket. Several tin cups, a washbasin, and a candleholder hung from a pack on his back. They bumped against each other as he walked.

Anna waved. "Hello, Gustaf! This is my cousin Kirsten. Her family arrived last month. Kirsten, Gustaf is a tinsmith."

"That I am," the old man said. The lines in his weather-beaten face deepened into a smile. "If your family needs a washtub, I can make it. If your cup leaks, I can fix it."

Kirsten knew that her family couldn't afford either of those things, not now, but she couldn't help smiling back. "I'm glad to meet you."

When Anna led the way inside, Kirsten could see that the tinsmith was an old friend. *"Välkommen!"* Uncle Olav said.

After introductions and greetings were exchanged, Aunt Inger motioned Gustaf to a seat. "You have a talent for arriving at meal-time," she teased, passing him a bowl.

"Well, it wouldn't suit to start right in with business," Gustaf said happily.

"Do you bring any news?" Uncle Olav asked.

Gustaf shook his head. "None to speak of. And though I stopped at Maryville this morning, I've almost no mail, either."

"Reverend Trulsson brought mail out just three days ago," Aunt Inger told him.

"That explains it, then." The old man nodded. "All I've got is a letter for Erik Sandahl."

The room went very still. Kirsten saw Papa's jaw tighten. Lars put down his spoon.

"I thought I might find him here," Gustaf was saying. Then he realized that something was wrong. "What?"

"Erik has disappeared," Uncle Olav said. His voice flat, he told the peddler what had happened.

The old man shook his head. "That's an awful shame. I remember those beasts of yours. Fine animals. What do you think I should do with Erik's letter?" He fetched the envelope from his pack and gave it to Uncle Olav. It was small, with a tiny bump in one corner.

"Did it come from Sweden?" Kirsten asked, longing to see what was inside.

Uncle Olav examined the stamp. "No, just from Saint Paul."

"Well, open it!" Papa said.

Uncle Olav frowned, turning the envelope over in his hands. "I don't feel right doing that."

"Why not?" Papa demanded. "Erik is gone!"

"Mail is private property," Uncle Olav said stubbornly.

"Starke and Fläckis were private property as well," Papa reminded his brother. Kirsten heard the frustration simmering behind the words. "There may be something in that letter that would tell us why Erik disappeared. If so, we have the right to know!" He banged one hand down on the table so hard that the silverware rattled.

Anna's face puckered, and her eyes brimmed with tears. Kirsten reached beneath the table and squeezed her young cousin's hand, but her gaze was locked on Uncle Olav.

Uncle Olav stared at the envelope for another long, silent moment before sliding one finger beneath its flap. He pulled the envelope open and reached inside. Then he pulled his hand free and peered inside.

"What's the matter?" Papa asked.

Uncle Olav tipped the envelope upside down. Something small fell to the table. Kirsten leaned over for a better look as a white button quivered to stillness beside the bread plate.

"That's it?" Papa growled. "No letter?"

"No letter," Uncle Olav said.

"Why would anyone mail a button?" Lars exclaimed.

Aunt Inger shook her head. "I don't know what to make of that."

Papa's jaw remained clenched tight. Everyone fell silent when he got to his feet and walked out of the cabin.

Mama started to get up, too. "I'll talk to him," she murmured.

Aunt Inger put a hand on Mama's arm. "Perhaps you should finish supper first," she said quietly. "Give him a chance to cool off." Mama nodded and sat back down, but she didn't reach for her spoon.

Kirsten wasn't hungry, either. She picked up the button and turned it over in her fingers. The button was made of some glossy material, perhaps pearl. Kirsten had never owned such a fine thing, so she couldn't be sure. What the button was made of, though, hardly mattered beside the larger questions: Who had sent Erik an envelope with nothing but a button inside? And *why?*

❤

After the dinner dishes were done and Gustav had settled down to mend a tin bucket of Aunt Inger's, Mama and Kirsten walked back to their cabin. "Kirsten," Mama said, "you saw the lovely yarn Mrs. Vanstrum gave me. You're old enough to start learning how to use two colors in your knitting. Fetch your needles and I'll get you started."

Kirsten hadn't been expecting that. She was tired, and her mind was tumbling with images of two huge oxen and one tiny button. Papa had not come back inside to eat supper, and even now the sound of his ax rang through the evening as he chopped firewood. Everything was going wrong—the last thing she felt like doing was knitting! Something in Mama's tone, though, made Kirsten swallow her objections.

They settled together on a bench just outside their front door. Mama often created snowflakes and roses on the socks and mittens that grew from her needles. Kirsten had learned to knit plain stockings back in Sweden, although she still needed help forming the heels properly. Now Mama showed Kirsten how to handle two balls of yarn. "Take six stitches with the white, then pick up the gray," she said. "Careful! Keep the unused color loose, or the work will pucker."

By the time whippoorwills began their evening calls, Kirsten was ready to throw her knitting on the ground. The wool stuck to her sweaty fingers, stitches slipped from the needles, and the two strands of yarn insisted on tangling themselves into knots. "Mama," she said finally, "can we stop now? I'm too tired to try anymore. We have lots of time before winter comes, anyway."

Mama smiled. "Yes, which will give you lots of time to practice."

"Maybe . . . maybe we shouldn't worry about fancywork right now," Kirsten suggested. "Since we're so busy."

For a long moment Mama didn't answer. Finally she said, "I just want us all to be happy here."

Kirsten didn't know what to say. Did the family's happiness depend on her knitting? "We will be, Mama," she said, although she added silently, *At least, I hope we will.*

"You've had a long day," Mama said. "Go on and get ready for bed."

She suddenly sounded so tired and sad that Kirsten's heart squeezed into a tight, hard ball. "I'll try again tomorrow," she promised.

Inside the cabin, Peter and Lars were already asleep. The Larsons often kept their window closed, preferring stuffy air to clouds of mosquitoes. This night was so sticky-hot, though, that Kirsten decided to open the window a few inches. She made a small smudge fire of green leaves in a bucket near her bed to discourage insects. She had just slipped beneath the sheet when she heard the murmur of voices outside.

"I was getting worried." That was Mama.

"I shouldn't have stomped out like that," Papa said. Kirsten imagined her parents sitting on the bench outside, Mama's hands busy with her knitting, Papa's hands still.

"We crossed an ocean to join Olav and his family," Mama said. "I'd hate to see you let a disagreement come between you and your brother."

"I'm just so frustrated!" Papa said. "I couldn't sit meekly at the table and pretend that everything was fine."

"Being angry at Olav won't bring the oxen back," Mama observed gently.

"I know," Papa admitted. "Olav made a mistake in trusting that boy... but I'm more worried than angry, I guess. Olav wouldn't have spent so much money on seed wheat if we hadn't been coming. If we lose the crop, or even part of it... I don't know how we'll manage."

Kirsten pulled the sheet over her head, not wanting to hear any more. All she wanted to do was sleep.

Instead, her mind kept trying to make sense of the strange "letter." Had the woman in the photograph sent Erik the button? Was it a clue to his disappearance? If so, why had Erik left *before* it arrived?

She was still awake when her parents came inside and went to bed. Some time later she heard the buzzing whine of a mosquito beneath the sheet. Slapping at the annoyance, Kirsten got out of bed. A haze of smoke still hung in the cabin, stinging her eyes, but the little smudge fire she'd built had gone out. If she didn't close the window, the air would be thick with mosquitoes by dawn.

She padded to the window. Before she could close it, though, she froze. In the moonlight she saw several dark shapes trot past the cabin. The wolves were back.

Suddenly a wolf face appeared on the other side of the glass, inches from her own. One massive front paw thrust through the opening, brushing against her arm.

"Papa!" Kirsten screamed, stumbling back from the wall.

Everyone came awake with startled cries. Papa appeared beside her in his long nightshirt. "What? What's wrong?"

"A wolf!" Kirsten pointed to the window with a trembling finger. "I got up to close the window, and suddenly there was a wolf, right there, looking at me!" She shuddered, remembering the wolf's massive head, the pointed nose, the glint of two dark eyes.

"I want to see the wolf!" Peter cried eagerly, while Lars asked, "Should we try to shoot it?"

"Hush," Mama said. "You boys go back to bed."

Papa closed the window with a resounding *thunk* and peered out. "It's gone," he reported. "I've heard that wolves sometimes stand on their hind legs and look in windows, but I didn't really believe it."

"*I* believe it," Kirsten said fervently. She was still trembling.

"I guess the wolves are curious about us." Papa tousled her hair. "Don't lose heart, daughter. You're safe."

Right at the moment, in the middle of the night, in the middle of a strange new country, Kirsten didn't feel safe at all. After Papa went back to bed, Mama sat with Kirsten, hugging her close. Kirsten slowly felt her trembles fade away. After a while, Mama kissed her forehead and tiptoed back to bed.

Kirsten rolled onto one side so that her back was to the window. She wanted to make Papa proud, and Mama too. If only she didn't feel so . . . so helpless! That was the problem.

So, what else can you do? Kirsten asked herself. She couldn't do anything about the wolves that roamed Minnesota. That left her with nothing to think about but her attempts to discover where Erik had gone. Once again, Kirsten sorted through what she knew, what she'd already done, who she'd talked to. What was left?

No one's talked to the Berg brothers, she thought. Little Berg was probably only a few years older than Erik. Perhaps Erik had confided in him.

And what about Mr. Green? He had a temper. He'd forced Johanna and Mrs. Green to walk home in the middle of the night. And a lot of things didn't feel quite right at the Green farm. Was Johanna's father hiding something?

Kirsten didn't like the idea of approaching either of those men. They both still felt like strangers. *But I need to talk to them,* Kirsten told herself. With that resolve, she settled down on her pillow. She wasn't out of ideas, not yet.

8
Surprise in the Root Cellar

After a quick breakfast the Larsons waved good-bye to Gustaf, who walked away with his dangling tinware clinking. Then they stretched aching muscles, straightened tired shoulders, and faced what needed to be done. They'd managed to get most of the grain cut, but they had at least one more long day of harvest ahead of them. Kirsten didn't let herself think about what came later—the hauling and threshing and milling, all without their oxen.

As she headed to the stable to milk the cows, she snatched a moment with her older brother. "Lars," she began, "is it far to the Berg brothers' place?"

"Why do you want to know?" Lars settled

his sweat-stained hat on his head. "You planning on going calling?"

"I was just wondering, that's all." Kirsten kicked a pebble ahead of her.

Lars's expression sharpened from curiosity to suspicion. "Why?"

Brothers! "All right, I'll tell you!" Kirsten said. "I've been trying to figure out why Erik left and where he went. Maybe Erik told one of the Bergs something that might give us a clue."

"If Erik had told anyone, I would have thought he'd tell me," Lars said stiffly.

Kirsten remembered Lars and Erik laughing as they mucked out stalls, telling stories after supper, hoisting a log together so they could carry it on their shoulders. "I'm sorry, Lars," she said. "But will you help me? It may be too late to get Starke and Fläckis back, but—but Erik owes us an explanation."

They had reached the stable. Lars stared toward the field where Papa and Uncle Olav were already at work. The sky was clouding over, which brought some welcome relief from the sun and heat—but the clouds brought more worry, too.

"The Berg brothers live several miles from here," Lars said finally. "It would take half the morning to walk there, talk to them, and get back. And you know Papa needs us here."

Kirsten hung her head. Lars's gloomy mood was contagious. "I *know* it's important that we finish harvesting the grain as quickly as we can," she muttered. "But every day that passes means Erik's probably farther away. That means we'll never get the oxen back, and Papa will stay angry at Uncle Olav, and Mama will get sadder, and—and the wolves will keep coming to our cabin at night, and—" *And the amber heart Mormor gave me is gone!* Kirsten had started to say. She swallowed the words, but her eyes filled with tears. "I wish we'd never left Sweden!"

She immediately regretted her outburst. "Please don't tell Papa I said that," she said, wiping her eyes. Her brother didn't answer. "Lars?"

He had turned away from her and was shielding his eyes with one hand. "It looks as if we have more company." His tone had changed.

Kirsten followed his gaze. The Berg brothers had emerged from the trees, each with a scythe balanced over one shoulder. *"God morgon!"* Big Berg called as they neared Lars and Kirsten.

"The Vanstrums told us what happened," Little Berg added. "We finished our harvest yesterday, so we're here to help."

Without another word, they walked on to the field. Lars whooped with joy and bounded after them.

"Tack!" Kirsten called. She didn't know whether to laugh or cry! She watched Papa and Uncle Olav pause when they noticed the newcomers. After a round of handshakes and shoulder slaps, the men settled down to work.

❤

The Berg brothers, both big and powerful men, handled their heavy scythes with ease.

Their shirts were soon dark with sweat, and flecks of straw clung to the damp skin on their forearms, but they kept moving. And with their help, the Larsons' wheat was all cut by midday.

"I can't believe it's done!" Kirsten exclaimed, surveying the field. Tidy bundles of grain dotted acres of stubble, where just days ago the wheat stalks had rippled like a golden ocean. The grain was all cut—and now, if she was lucky, she'd have a chance to talk to Little Berg about Erik.

"The job's not done until the grain is well dried and safe in the barn," Uncle Olav reminded her.

Aunt Inger pushed back her sunbonnet and wiped her forehead. "True enough. But for now, I think we should celebrate what *has* been accomplished. Let's start with a good meal."

At the house, Kirsten helped prepare a hearty dinner. They ate outside to escape the stove's heat. When she saw Little Berg pull his pipe from a vest pocket and wander a short distance away, she knew she needed to seize the opportunity. But what excuse could she have for approaching him? Kirsten looked around urgently for inspiration—and found it. She grabbed the coffeepot and a mug and followed Little Berg. Then she forced herself to look up into his eyes. *"Kaffe?"* she asked.

"Ja!" He grinned, tucking his pipe away again. "My brother and I just have *kaffe* on Sundays."

He held the cup while Kirsten carefully poured. Then he sniffed the steaming black liquid happily. "Ah. Inger makes good *kaffe.*"

Kirsten set the heavy pot on the ground and took a deep breath. "Mr. Berg, may I ask you something?"

"Of course!"

"I keep wondering about Erik," Kirsten said. "I thought you might have an idea about where he went."

Little Berg looked shocked. *"Me?"*

Kirsten balled her skirt in her hands. "I don't mean to say that you know where he is," she said hastily. "I just meant that, well, you knew Erik longer than we did. Did he ever say anything that might give us a clue? Did he dream about heading west?"

"Nej." Little Berg waved a hand. "I never heard him say anything like that. Erik liked that piece of land he'd claimed. He worked hard to improve it. We had no idea he was thinking of running off."

"Do you think Erik wanted to get married?" Kirsten asked. "Did he ever mention a sweetheart?"

"Can't say that I ever heard Erik mention a girl that way." Little Berg scratched his ear. "I don't think he even wanted to marry."

"Didn't *want* to?" Kirsten asked, surprised.

"Once Erik teased my brother and me about our place. Said it was too rough and needed a woman's touch. I said, 'How about you? That shanty of yours is desperate for a good housekeeper. And having a good cook around wouldn't do you any harm either.'" Little Berg looked down at Kirsten. "My brother is a pretty good cook," he told her, "but Erik could hardly boil potatoes."

"And what did Erik say to that?"

"Well, he got quiet," Little Berg said. "Then he muttered something like, 'I do just fine on my own. You can't depend on women anyway. They're too fickle.'"

"Fickle?" Kirsten wrinkled her nose.

"You know—unreliable," Little Berg told her. "Erik meant that women change their minds too often." He grinned. "Now, don't tell your mama or Inger that I said that, though. Right?"

Kirsten agreed absently. Her mind was already trying to knit this new strand of information into a design. Had Erik been thinking of the woman in the photograph when he said that women were fickle? Had she promised to marry him and then run off with someone else? Had Erik decided to try to win her back with stolen gifts?

Kirsten touched her throat, longing to feel the smooth comfort of Mormor's gift. Perhaps it would be better if she *didn't* figure out where Erik had gone. If he had stolen her amber heart, she could never forgive him.

❤

Kirsten, Lisbeth, and Anna spent the rest of the afternoon working in the garden. Then Kirsten's family had a simple supper of bread and cheese. As Kirsten tossed a basin of dishwater outside, she glanced up at the sky. Thanks to the Berg brothers, the day's chores had been finished with a couple of hours of daylight left. *This is the best opportunity to visit the Green farm I'm likely to get,* she thought.

Before Kirsten could ask permission to go, however, Mama turned to her with a smile. "Let's fetch our knitting, Kirsten."

"But—but I was hoping to visit Johanna!" Kirsten blurted. She felt horrible as she watched Mama's smile fade, but asking Mr. Green about Erik was Kirsten's last idea. If there was any faint chance left of finding Erik, and perhaps even of getting Starke and Fläckis back, she had to do this *now.*

"I see," Mama said quietly. "Well, I suppose that would be all right. Just be sure to get home before dark."

Kirsten blew out the breath she'd been holding. "Thank you, Mama. I'll be home long before dark."

Kirsten hurried along the trail to the Green farm. Even though the sun had not yet set, a candle-lantern had been lit and placed in one window of the Greens' cabin. Mama would have clucked over such an extravagance, but Kirsten appreciated the tiny flicker of welcome.

As she walked to the front step, Mrs. Green appeared. "Oh—Kirsten, it's you." She managed a smile, but her shoulders sagged with apparent disappointment.

Kirsten hesitated, feeling suddenly uncertain. "Johanna invited me to come back. I hope you don't mind."

"Of course not! Of course not, dear," Mrs. Green said quickly, although she seemed to be looking over Kirsten's shoulder. "How lovely that you've come. Johanna's so often lonely."

"Kirsten!" Johanna called. She stood by the stable, beckoning happily. Kirsten ran to meet her. "I was cleaning the stable when I heard your voice," Johanna told her.

"Is your father here?" Kirsten asked.

"No, he went hunting this afternoon." Johanna squeezed Kirsten's hand. "Would you like to try riding Svarten today?"

Since she couldn't talk with Johanna's father anyway, Kirsten accepted the invitation. Svarten was as gentle as Johanna had claimed. Once Kirsten got used to being on the horse's back, she loved guiding him in circles around the yard.

"You can have a longer ride another day," Johanna said finally. "I need to check on Mama before I start milking."

Kirsten slid to the ground reluctantly and paused to pat Svarten's neck. *"Tack,"* she whispered, wishing again—just for a moment!—that her family could afford such a beautiful creature.

As she followed Johanna toward the cabin, though, Kirsten put her mind on more important things. The sun was sinking behind the trees. If Mr. Green didn't return soon, she'd have to head home without talking to him.

Mrs. Green was waiting for them. "Girls, come inside," she said. "Quickly, now."

Kirsten cast a glance at the shadows lengthening across the yard. *I'll wait just a few more minutes,* she decided. She followed Johanna into the cabin.

Mrs. Green stayed in the doorway, looking out at the woods. "Johanna, don't you think your father should be home by now?"

"He'll be along soon, Mama," Johanna said. "I'm sure of it. Kirsten, would you like a *smörgås?"*

"All right," Kirsten said. She wasn't hungry, but she wanted to be polite. "Then I'll have to start for home."

Johanna soon had three places set at the table. "Come sit down, Mama," she called.

Mrs. Green didn't move. Through the open

door, Kirsten heard an evening bird begin to call its name. *Whip-poor-will!*

Johanna raised her voice. "Mama? Are you coming?"

"I'm not hungry," Mrs. Green said.

Kirsten slid onto a bench and dutifully spread some jam on a slice of bread, but she was growing increasingly uneasy. She could hear the Greens' cow in the stable, lowing to be milked. Johanna's good spirits had fled, and her mother looked ready to jump out of her skin.

Whip-poor-will! Whip-poor-will! A second bird answered the call now. Mrs. Green flinched. "Something's happened to your father," she told Johanna, hunching her shoulders as if fearing a blow.

A tingle danced over Kirsten's skin. Something felt very wrong.

Johanna went to the door and took her mother's arm. "Come away from the door," she said gently. "I brought more water in earlier. Why don't you scrub the floor? Papa will be home soon—"

Johanna's soothing tone was interrupted by another bird, quite close. *Whip-poor-will! Whip-poor-will!*

Mrs. Green burst into tears. "I hate those birds!" she cried. "You hear it, don't you, Kirsten? They're saying, *'Oh, he's killed! Oh, he's killed!'*"

Kirsten stared at Mrs. Green. She had no idea what to say or what to do.

Mrs. Green hugged her arms across her chest, looking from one girl to the other as tears ran down her cheeks. "Don't you hear it?" she repeated, whispering now.

Johanna tugged her mother away from the door. "Mama, come—sit—*down,*" she said firmly. She managed to get her mother into a chair, but Mrs. Green continued to weep.

Kirsten wanted to help, but she didn't know how. "What can I do?"

"Could you milk the cow for me?" Johanna asked. "I can't leave Mama when she's like this."

"Of course," Kirsten assured her, although her heart sank at the idea. It would be fully dark by the time she finished that chore.

"You can take the lantern." Johanna quickly lit a second candle, then handed the tin lantern to Kirsten.

Outside, the sky's evening blue was streaked with dark purple. Kirsten forced down a quiver of panic. *One thing at a time,* she told herself, and hurried to the stable.

As Kirsten settled down on the low milking stool, Johanna's cow mooed a complaint, as if to say, *You're late!* "Sorry, girl," Kirsten whispered. She leaned her cheek against the cow's belly as she milked, pretending it was Kulla. Through the stable door she could hear the whippoor-wills, still calling. Since arriving in Minnesota, Kirsten had come to like the sound, since it signaled twilight and an end to the day's chores. Suddenly, though, the birds' calls *did* sound mournful. She shuddered, remembering the haunted look in Mrs. Green's eyes.

After stripping the cow dry, Kirsten strained the milk through a piece of loosely woven linen that she found hanging from a nail. Johanna probably kept her separating pans in the root cellar where the milk would stay cool, just as the Larsons did. With the heavy bucket in one hand and the lantern in the other, Kirsten walked quickly to the root cellar behind the cabin, unlatched the door, and went inside.

The earthen-walled cellar was pitch-black. Kirsten gratefully hung the lantern from a convenient hook in one of the wooden beams supporting the roof. There—the pans she needed were stacked on a shelf. Kirsten soon had the milk set out so that the thick cream could rise, ready to be skimmed and churned into butter.

That accomplished, Kirsten wiped her hands on her skirt and paused. She probably should go back to the cabin . . . but Mrs. Green's tears, and her insistence that the birds were predicting a death, made Kirsten feel helpless, and a little embarrassed, too. Besides, Kirsten's own mama was no doubt wondering where she was. The thought of setting out alone in the dark, though, sent shivers rippling down Kirsten's backbone.

As she glanced around the small, dank room,

trying to decide what to do, Kirsten suddenly noticed an unexpected glint on a shelf near the door. What could that be? She pushed aside some turnips and was surprised to find a second lantern, and even three precious matches. Matches cost five cents apiece! Had Johanna forgotten that she had matches on the day she'd come to borrow coals? Or had she and her mother decided to save these matches for . . . for *what?*

Before she could puzzle that out, Kirsten noticed something else unexpected, tucked farther back in the shadows. Leaning over a bin of onions, she picked up the wooden *tine* she'd admired the day before, sweetly carved with Johanna's initials.

What was Johanna's trinket box doing in the root cellar? Yesterday it had sat in a place of honor on the shelf inside the cabin. Kirsten remembered how Johanna had protectively moved the *tine* away from the edge.

Or . . . had she been moving the *tine* away from Kirsten?

Kirsten stared at the box for a long moment before her curiosity triumphed. After glancing toward the door, she set the box on an empty shelf and put the lantern she'd brought beside it. Then she pulled off the lid—and gasped.

9
Anna Provides a Clue

Kirsten's fingers trembled as she slowly pulled a familiar black ribbon from the *tine.* Her amber heart gleamed in the faint light. Mormor's gift! Kirsten slipped the ribbon over her neck and let the heart slide beneath her dress, smooth and warm, like a hug from her grandmother. Tears burned Kirsten's eyes and she blinked hard, not sure if they came from her relief at finding her treasure . . . or the sickening realization that she'd found her treasure in Johanna's *tine.*

And that wasn't all. Mrs. Vanstrum's blue rosette was in the *tine,* too. Kirsten quickly tucked it into her pocket. There was also a brooch with a lock of hair enclosed in glass, and a scrap of lace, and . . . what was this, on the bottom? Kirsten felt a hard lump beneath coarse paper—

"Johanna?" The man's voice was so unexpected, and so close, that Kirsten gave a cry of alarm. She whirled to see Mr. Green standing in the root cellar's doorway. "What are *you* doing here?" he demanded angrily. He held a musket, and even in the dim light Kirsten could see his fingers tighten on the stock.

Kirsten's mouth went dry. She was trapped! "I—I . . ."

Then Johanna's voice came from outside. "Papa?"

Mr. Green turned and disappeared into the night. Kirsten grabbed the lantern and ran outside after him. He headed straight toward the cabin, though, and she veered to the side. "Kirsten?" Johanna called from the back door, but Kirsten didn't stop.

As soon as she left the farmyard, Kirsten plunged onto the dark forest path. *Slow down,* she cautioned herself. Although the lantern shielded the candle, the flame had flickered wildly as she ran. The night was black as velvet now. She had none of those precious matches. No matter what else happened, she must *not* let her candle go out.

Kirsten kept her gaze locked on the pale light cast on the ground by the lantern as she began walking home. She tried not to think about everything that had happened at the Green farm that evening, or of the wolves that stalked through these woods. Still, the night seemed full of strange rustles, and she imagined unseen eyes watching her pass.

She reached up to touch Mormor's amber heart—and only then realized that the items she'd found in the bottom of Johanna's *tine* were still clenched in her right hand. She didn't feel guilty about taking her amber heart or Mrs. Vanstrum's rosette. But who did the other things belong to—the brooch, and the lace, and the parcel? She'd have to sort that out later.

As she slipped the treasures into her pocket with the rosette, a faint sound made her pause.

She thought she'd heard . . . Yes! Someone was calling her name. *"Kir-sten! Kir-sten!"*

"Here!" she hollered. "Papa, I'm here!"

A few moments later she saw the tiny bob of another lantern through the trees. When Papa appeared on the path, she put down her own light and ran into his arms. The crush of his hug felt wonderful. *Safe.* She was safe. And Papa could help make sense of everything that had happened.

After a moment, though, Papa gently pushed her back so that he could look her in the eye. "Where have you been?" he asked sternly. "Mama told you to be home before dark!"

"I wanted to, Papa," Kirsten began. "But Mr. Green wasn't home and Mrs. Green got very upset, and so I stayed to help—"

"Didn't you think about your own mama? She's terribly worried!" Papa shook his head. "Come along, Kirsten. Your mother deserves an apology."

They walked the rest of the way home in silence. Kirsten was still glad to have her father beside her. But everything she'd wanted to tell him stayed unspoken, and a heavy sadness weighed on her shoulders. She had disappointed Papa again.

❤

In all the commotion of greeting her mother, saying she was sorry, being reminded that she had to return the Greens' lantern the next day, and being hustled off to bed, Kirsten could do nothing more than slip the items she'd taken from Johanna's *tine* under her mattress. Soon Papa and the boys settled down to sleep, but Mama returned to her knitting, hunching again near the tiny light of a grease-and-wick lamp.

Kirsten wasn't able to find sleep either. *Why* did Johanna have things that didn't belong to her? The question made Kirsten's heart ache. And why had Johanna hidden the *tine* in the root cellar? Was it so that no other curious visitors would ask about the pretty box and want to see what was inside?

Who did the brooch and the lace belong to? And what was in the little parcel? *You shouldn't have taken those things!* a voice in her head scolded. A second voice argued, *But I didn't* plan *to take them! I was holding them in my hand when Mr. Green scared me, and then . . .* Then she'd ended up bringing them home. Did that make *her* a thief? She hoped not.

Kirsten thought again about the little wrapped parcel, wishing she could get up and examine it. Mama would want to know what she was doing, though, and Kirsten didn't have enough answers to explain. Not yet, anyway. Looking at the parcel would have to wait for the morning.

❤

At daybreak, Kirsten quickly dressed. She was able to snatch the items she'd taken from Johanna's *tine* and slide them back into her apron pocket without anyone seeing. Papa stood staring out the doorway, an unhappy set to his mouth. "Feels like a storm coming," he muttered. "Lord help us if it rains."

Mama was laying kindling over the embers in the fireplace so that she could start breakfast. "I'll fetch some water," Kirsten volunteered. Mama nodded.

Kirsten grabbed two buckets and hurried to the stream. Once there, she plopped onto a fallen log and pulled the parcel from her pocket. It was an envelope of sorts, made from heavy brown paper and tied with string.

And written on the front, in Swedish and what must be English, were the words *Erik Sandahl, near Maryville, Minnesota.*

Kirsten stared at the address, hardly able to believe her eyes. More mail for Erik? What was the parcel doing in Johanna's *tine?* She fingered the lump in one corner. It was larger than a button. Her fingers itched to open the envelope! But she paused, remembering how Papa and Uncle Olav had argued about whether they should open the envelope that Gustaf the tinsmith had delivered. This was too big a decision to make by herself. *I'll ask Lisbeth for advice,* she thought.

A chickadee called a cheerful good morning from a nearby branch, reminding Kirsten that Mama would be expecting the water. After tucking the package away, she filled her buckets and headed back to the cabin.

❤

Kirsten didn't have a chance to talk with Lisbeth until early afternoon. Aunt Inger had settled in the shade of a big oak tree with some mending, and Mama joined her, knitting needles in hand.

"Those plums I picked need to be cooked," Lisbeth said. "I should start that before the day gets any hotter."

"I'll help," Kirsten said quickly.

"Me, too!" Anna announced, following the older girls into the house. "I love plums!"

"I need to talk with Lisbeth privately," Kirsten told her. "Do you mind, Anna? I'm sure

Peter would be glad to play with you outside." Anna and Peter were the only people who weren't exhausted from the wheat harvest.

"I don't want to play outside," Anna protested. "Why are you two keeping secrets?"

Lisbeth fetched the fruit and a clean kettle. "Go outside," she told her sister. Anna frowned, but she turned and flounced out the door.

"Now," Lisbeth said. "What's happened?"

The two girls settled at the big table. While Lisbeth picked over the fruit, cutting out bad spots and pits, Kirsten described everything that had taken place at the Greens' farm. Her cousin blinked with disbelief when Kirsten told her what she'd found in the root cellar. "Your amber heart was in the *tine?*" Lisbeth repeated slowly. "You think *Johanna* took it? Oh my."

"I don't know what else to think!" Kirsten said miserably. "Mrs. Vanstrum's rosette was there, too, and a couple of other pretty things. And this." Kirsten pulled the parcel from her pocket and laid it on the table. "It's addressed to Erik. Do you think we should open it?"

Lisbeth stared at the parcel. "Oh, I don't know. Maybe you should talk to your parents about it."

"I wanted to, but . . ." Kirsten sighed. "Both of them are unhappy with me because I worried them last evening. And you saw how angry Papa got when we opened the last envelope, with nothing but the button inside!" She touched the hard lump in the parcel. "I don't know what this is, but—"

"You don't know what *what* is?" Anna asked as she came in the door. Kirsten quickly snatched the parcel and hid it on her lap, under the table.

"Anna, please go back outside," Lisbeth said.

"What's the big secret?" Anna demanded. "Why can't I see?" She snatched a plum slice, but juice dripped from her fingers before she could pop it into her mouth.

"Anna, that will stain Mama's rug!" Lisbeth cried. "Kirsten and I are having a private conversation, and you're being a pest. Go back outside!"

Lisbeth rarely raised her voice, and Anna's eyes glittered with tears as she turned and ran out the door. *"Sisters,"* Lisbeth said.

Kirsten quickly fetched a rag and wiped up a tiny spot on Aunt Inger's prized rug. "And brothers," she added, remembering how close Peter had come to overhearing her talk with Lisbeth in the stable. Then she settled down again. She and Lisbeth needed to make a decision before someone else came inside! "So," she said. "What do you think I should do?"

Lisbeth poured some water and honey into the kettle and began slowly mashing the fruit with a spoon. "I don't know why Johanna had this package, but it doesn't belong to her any more than it belongs to us. And I think your father was right. Erik left us with a huge problem. That parcel might give us some answers. I say, go ahead and open it."

Kirsten nodded. "If there's helpful information inside, I'll tell Papa." She carefully sliced the string with a knife, slid one finger under the flap, and broke the blobs of wax holding it closed. Then she turned the envelope upside down over her lap and caught what was inside.

"What is it?" Lisbeth demanded.

Kirsten held out her palm, displaying a rose-colored marble.

"There was no letter?"

"No letter," Kirsten said, shaking her head in frustration. "Just the marble. Why is someone sending Erik these things? *Why?* It makes no sense!"

"I can't imagine." Lisbeth stood and picked up the kettle, ready to carry it to the stove. "I simply can't—"

A high, frightened scream cut the words short.

"Anna!" Lisbeth dropped the kettle with a resounding crash and splatter and ran outside without a backward glance. Heart thumping, Kirsten raced after her.

They found Anna curled into a ball on the ground beside the garden fence. Peter crouched beside her, looking scared. "What happened?" Lisbeth cried. "Are you hurt?"

"I—I don't think so." Anna sat up gingerly. "Peter dared me to walk the fence rail. It cracked and I slipped off."

"Peter!" Kirsten scolded.

"She didn't have to do it," Peter protested.

Lisbeth pulled Anna into a hug. "You frightened me!" she exclaimed. "Don't ever do that again, either of you!"

Aunt Inger and Mama came running to join them. "What happened?" Aunt Inger asked, and the explanations began all over again. Aunt Inger inspected Anna. Mama gave Peter a talking-to.

Kirsten headed back to the house, but she stopped short when she saw that the kettle of plums and honey had landed on Aunt Inger's rug. "Oh no," Kirsten moaned. Would those stains ever come out?

She put some water over the fire to boil and set about cleaning up. Lisbeth would be horrified when she saw the mess. Kirsten shook her head as she thought how Anna's scream had made Lisbeth forget all the irritation she'd felt just a few moments earlier. Kirsten had experienced the same swings of emotion about Lars and Peter many times. The boys could be terribly annoying or hurt her feelings, and then she would wish that she didn't have any brothers! But when times got hard . . .

Kirsten went still as a new idea shot through her head. She picked up the marble she'd dropped when Anna screamed and rolled it around in her palm as she rolled the idea around in her mind.

Then she sprang to her feet and ran outside. "Everybody, come quick!" she called. "I think I've figured it out!"

10
Looking for Answers

Ten minutes later, everyone was gathered around the table in the big house. "Slow down," Papa told Kirsten, "and start again at the beginning."

Jiggling with excitement, Kirsten tried to organize her thoughts. "I've been trying to figure out where Erik went," she began. "The day I had to chase Kulla, she wandered almost all the way to his shanty, so I looked around inside. I found a photograph of a young woman, hidden away with one of the newspapers Reverend Trulsson had brought. One corner of the newspaper was missing, though. Erik probably took it with him."

Uncle Olav planted his hands on his knees. "I didn't know anything about this."

"Well, I didn't want to talk too much about it," Kirsten admitted. "Everyone seemed to think that looking for Erik was a waste of time. Mrs. Green gave me a copy of the newspaper, though." Kirsten retrieved the newspaper and handed it to Lisbeth. "Will you read the 'Notices' section again—the part that Erik tore out?"

As Lisbeth smoothed the thin newsprint open on the table, Kirsten glanced at the circle of faces. Lars, Peter, and Anna looked curious. Aunt Inger and Uncle Olav looked thoughtful. Mama was staring at her knitting, but Papa was frowning.

I hope I'm right, Kirsten thought, feeling a flutter of nervousness in her stomach.

Lisbeth began to read the notices aloud. "'The *Mary C.* reached our dock yesterday with a full freight for the merchants of Saint Paul . . . Sidewalks are now being laid near the Post Office, an improvement long needed . . . Notice: Whereas my wife, Sally Braxton, has without just cause left my home, I hereby forbid all persons from sheltering her or trusting her on my account . . . Wanted: A man to build a fence around two village lots—'"

Kirsten held up a hand. "Stop there," she told Lisbeth. Then she faced the others. "At first, I wondered if Erik had hurried to Saint Paul so he could get the fencing job. That didn't seem likely, though. Why take a temporary job when he had lumber at his shanty that he could sell?"

Papa drummed one thumb on the table. "So this doesn't tell us anything."

"I think it does." Kirsten took a deep breath. "I think that third notice is the one that sent Erik to Saint Paul. The one about a wife who left her husband."

"That makes no sense!" Lars scoffed.

Mama put her knitting down. "Kirsten, it was sweet of you to try to find Erik. But I don't understand what a woman leaving her husband has to do with him."

"I think the woman is Erik's *sister,*" Kirsten explained. "Remember when Miss Mobeck asked him if he had immigrated alone? He said something about not having 'any real family here in the Maryville district.'"

"That doesn't mean he has a sister in Saint Paul!" Lars protested.

"No," Kirsten admitted. "But Erik has gotten two pieces of mail in just the few days since he disappeared. One held that button. The Greens were keeping another little parcel"—she glided over that information quickly, hoping no one would ask about it—"and that one held this." She displayed the marble for everyone to see.

"This marble looks just like one of Erik's marbles, which were a gift from his father," Kirsten went on. "I'm guessing that Erik's sister got several marbles at the same time he did. Maybe she mailed one to Erik as a signal! It might have been her way of letting him know that she was in trouble and needed help."

"What about the button?" Peter asked.

"Well . . . I haven't figured that out," Kirsten confessed. "It might have been a signal, too."

"So you think this Sally Braxton is Erik's sister?" Lisbeth asked. "Sally isn't a common Swedish name."

"No, but perhaps she changed it! Just like the Greens changed their last name. To be more American."

"I don't know," Aunt Inger said slowly. "I suppose that could be one possible explanation, but . . . I don't know."

"Well, here's what we do know," Kirsten said. "Erik was proud of his land claim, and he worked hard to improve it. Erik once told Little Berg that women are fickle." She leaned forward, eager to convince them. "I thought that maybe the photograph was of a lady who had broken Erik's heart. But maybe Erik was talking about a sister!"

Lars waved away a bee that had flown in through the open door. "I never heard him mention a sister."

"Neither did I," Anna added.

"But you're the one who made me think of it," Kirsten told Anna. "Lisbeth scolded you this afternoon for pestering us, and for dripping plum juice, right?"

Anna glanced guiltily at her mother's rug, soaking in a washtub, before whispering, *"Ja."*

"But when Lisbeth heard you scream, she dropped the kettle and ran. Nothing else mattered but making sure that you were all right. Don't you see?" She looked around the table. "Uncle Olav believed Erik was trustworthy. So, what would make Erik run off without a word of explanation? What would make Erik leave us holding the loan? It would have to be something very important." Kirsten nodded at Anna. "Like having a sister who needed help."

For a long moment no one spoke. "You know," Uncle Olav said finally, "Kirsten might be right."

Papa rubbed his chin. "We could probably find out. But it would take several days to get to Saint Paul, make inquiries, and get back."

"Well, we can't get the wheat in until it dries anyway," Uncle Olav said. "And the Bergs have already offered to help."

"I'll keep an eye on it while you're gone," Lars promised.

"And if it needs to be moved to the barn before you return, we'll get it done," Aunt Inger said stoutly.

"Going to Saint Paul is worth a try." Uncle Olav slapped a hand on the table, looking at his brother. "And if Erik *is* in the city, dealing with a sister's American husband, and lawyers, he might need some help. Let's get moving."

Kirsten bounced on her toes. Papa warned, "Don't get your hopes too high. This might be a fool's errand."

She nodded, half happy and half anxious. She didn't know if the men would bring Erik back from Saint Paul, but maybe—just maybe—they'd come back with some answers.

❤

Kirsten's high spirits sagged after the men left, when she faced the prospect of returning the Greens' lantern. And what about the brooch and the piece of lace? Had they been stolen from someone too, or did they belong to Johanna? Kirsten felt her heart ache again as she tried to picture her friend hiding things that did not belong to her. Kirsten simply couldn't imagine it. *I need to talk with Johanna about this,* she thought, and felt a little better. And maybe Mama would go to the Green farm with her! Mama would surely know how to help Mrs. Green with her worries.

When Kirsten entered the cabin, though, she saw Mama sitting by the window, rereading Mormor's letter. Mama's cheeks were tear-stained, although she managed a smile. "Yes, Kirsten? Were you looking for me?"

Kirsten hesitated. "Would you like to come with me when I return the Greens' lantern? Mrs. Green seems . . ." She tried to find the right words. "Mrs. Green got very anxious yesterday. The whippoorwills upset her, and I didn't know how to help."

"I'm afraid I wouldn't be good company for her today." Mama sighed. "Please give her my regards and tell her I'll come visit soon."

Kirsten nodded, trying to hide her disappointment.

"And remember," Mama added, "I expect you home well before dark!"

❤

When Kirsten reached the Green farm, she found the clearing quiet. No one was hoeing weeds in the garden; no one was cutting wheat. Just as Kirsten started to wonder if anyone was home, the cabin door opened. Johanna appeared, tossed a basin of dishwater into the yard, and then paused, shading her eyes from the sun. "Kirsten?" she called. "Is that you?"

Kirsten squared her shoulders and walked across the yard. "I brought back your lantern," she said. "And—and I need to talk to you. About this." She pulled her amber heart free, letting it dangle from its ribbon.

Johanna looked confused. "It's very pretty,

but why do you want to talk to me about it? Kirsten, what's wrong?"

"Don't you know?" Hurt made Kirsten's voice shake. "This has been missing since the night everyone was at our farm. I found your *tine* yesterday in the root cellar, Johanna. With my amber heart inside it."

Johanna's shoulders slowly slumped. She looked at her toes. "I hope you'll give me a chance to explain," she whispered finally. "My parents are visiting a neighbor, but maybe you should come inside."

Kirsten followed Johanna into the cabin, noticing again all the extra niceties. The Greens already had so many pretty things! How could Johanna explain taking *more* pretty things from other people?

Johanna sat down at the table, and Kirsten stiffly sat down opposite her. Johanna rested both elbows on the table and cradled her forehead in her hands. "It's hard to know where to begin," she said. "You saw how upset Mama got yesterday because Papa was late."

"Ja." Kirsten wondered what that had to do with stealing.

"Mama's had a very hard time. She didn't want to leave Sweden. I had an older sister, but she died, and Papa thought it would be best if we came to America and started a new life." Johanna looked Kirsten in the eye. "But Mama hates it here. She's terrified of the woods. Wolves come around the cabin at night."

A shiver rippled down Kirsten's back. That fear she understood all too well.

"Once a couple of lumberjacks spent the night here and got drunk," Johanna was saying. "That was scary. And Mama's never gotten used to seeing Indians. One time Mrs. Vanstrum came to visit, right after her baby was born. Papa was gone. I went berry-picking, and while I was away, an Indian lady came in. She kept pointing at the baby, and Mrs. Vanstrum and Mama got it into their heads that the Indian lady wanted to take the baby."

Kirsten gasped. "Take the baby?"

"That wasn't it at all!" Johanna said. "The

woman just wanted the baby's little knit booties. Mrs. Vanstrum finally figured that out and gave them to her, and she left. By the time I got back home, Mrs. Vanstrum was laughing about it. And the next day that Indian woman came back. She brought her own baby, wearing those booties, and she left the prettiest little beaded rattle. I gave it to Mrs. Vanstrum next time I saw her."

"So it was sort of a trade," Kirsten said.

"Yes. That's usually how it works. I've gotten used to the Indian people coming by. But Mama . . ." Johanna shook her head. "Mama never has. She doesn't like having peddlers come by, either. Or men looking for work, or newcomers needing a place to stay. Mama's gotten so terrified of strangers that Papa finally cut in the back door and put that latch you saw on the inside of the root cellar. Now, if Mama sees any stranger coming, she runs out the back and hides in the cellar."

Kirsten blew out a long, slow breath as she pictured poor Mrs. Green, fearfully locking herself into the damp root cellar. "That's why you keep a lantern there," she guessed.

"Right." Johanna nodded. "Papa thought that if we just helped Mama get used to living here, she'd calm down. But she hasn't. She's stopped working in the garden because she's afraid to be that far from the cabin. She forgets to fix supper, or to watch the fire. Sometimes she scrubs the floor all day, over and over, because it keeps her busy."

A deep, heavy sadness was growing in Kirsten's heart. "Where is your mother now?"

"Papa took her to visit a neighbor lady." Johanna managed a wan smile. "Your Aunt Inger has been very kind, but she's just so . . . so capable, you know?"

Kirsten nodded. She didn't think anything would discourage Aunt Inger.

"A German couple settled a mile or so away," Johanna continued. "Mr. Werner speaks a little English, but his wife speaks only German. She's having a hard time getting used to Minnesota, too. Even though she and Mama can't talk to each other, they like to spend time together. Once Mrs. Werner came here and just cried, and Mama patted her hand and made her tea. It's as if they understand each other, somehow. Papa took Mama over to the Werners' place today, hoping that would cheer her up."

"So maybe things are getting a little better?" Kirsten asked hopefully.

Johanna studied her fingers. "Not really. We've been trying to keep Mama's bad nerves a secret. That's why we left your farm that night. Papa was afraid that being around so many people would be a strain, and he wanted to head for home before something upset Mama. You saw how she gets. It doesn't take much anymore to set her off in a fit. Even a whippoorwill."

"Oh, Johanna," Kirsten said. "I'm so sorry."

Johanna gave a tiny, helpless shrug. "After that confusion with the baby's booties, I noticed that things started to disappear. One day, I found in the stable a pretty china cup that we'd brought from Sweden. When I asked Mama about it, she told me we had to hide it so that it wouldn't get stolen."

"So your mother..." Kirsten's voice trailed away. She remembered Mrs. Green worrying that someone might steal the beautiful blue sugar wrappers.

"I noticed last night that my *tine* was missing," Johanna said. "I knew I'd find it somewhere. I didn't know Mama had taken your necklace, Kirsten! But I'm sure that's what happened."

Kirsten nodded. Johanna was no doubt right.

"Please believe me!" Johanna's voice was pleading. "Mama didn't mean any harm. I think that when she saw something so pretty, she just decided it needed to be tucked away to keep it safe."

"I *do* believe you," Kirsten said. After all, she'd seen Mrs. Green reduced to tears by a bird's call. "But you need to know that I found some other things in the *tine,* too." She began pulling the items from her pocket. "This rosette belongs to Mrs. Vanstrum."

Johanna sighed. "I'll give it back to her and explain. I think she'll understand."

"And there were these two things." Kirsten placed the brooch and the piece of lace on the table.

"Those are mine." Johanna picked them up and cradled them gently in her palm. "The brooch was made with a lock of my sister's hair. And she made the lace."

"Then I know how precious those things are," Kirsten said sympathetically. "The only other thing in the *tine* was something strange. A little parcel for Erik. It was similar to another one I saw that was also addressed to him. Where do you suppose your mother would have gotten that?"

Johanna twisted her mouth, thinking. "All I can imagine is that Mr. Werner happened to pick up mail in town one day. If Mama saw the package for Erik at the Werners' house, she might have brought it home with her."

"That makes sense." Kirsten reached across the table and squeezed her friend's hand. "I'm truly sorry about your mother. But I'm glad to know what's happening, too. Now, if I only knew for sure about those packages for Erik!"

A male voice spoke from the doorway. "Packages for me?"

11
The Wolf

"Erik!" Kirsten squealed. She jumped up so fast that the bench toppled over. Johanna ran to wrap Erik in a hug.

Erik's worn clothes were dusty. His face had a strained look Kirsten didn't remember, and he looked as tired as she'd felt after a hot day in the wheat field. His smile, though, was as warm as ever. "Hello, girls."

"We didn't know where you'd gone!" Johanna told him, sniffling a little.

"Where are your parents?" Erik asked her.

"Papa walked Mama over to the Werners'."

"Your mama had another bad spell?" he asked. "I'm sorry I haven't been around to help. I'll try to make up for it." He looked over Johanna's shoulder at Kirsten. "And I know that I have some explaining to do at your place, too."

"A lot," Kirsten agreed soberly. "Did you know about Starke and Fläckis?"

He frowned. "What about them?"

When Kirsten described the sheriff's visit, Erik sank into a chair and buried his face in his hands. "Oh, no!" he moaned. "I thought I had more time. I hurried home as quickly as I could . . . Oh, this is *terrible!* I've got to go talk to Olav right away!"

"Uncle Olav and Papa headed to Saint Paul this afternoon to look for you," Kirsten told him. "I'm surprised you didn't see them on the road!"

"I must have just missed them," Erik said. "I went straight home to the shanty. Then I came here to see if things were all right. Your place was my next stop."

"But where did you *go?*" Johanna demanded.

Erik scrubbed his face with his palms. "It's a long story."

"I think I've guessed some of it," Kirsten

told him. "Did you go to Saint Paul to look for your sister?"

He lifted his head and gaped at her. "How on earth did you know that?"

Kirsten told Erik and Johanna what she'd found, heard, and guessed. "You've just about got it," Erik admitted. "I came to this country with my sister, Sigrid. We had to work our way across the country, but our dream was to start a farm here in Minnesota, together. Then Sigrid met an American man in Saint Paul and quickly fell in love with him. Tom Braxton. I didn't like him. And I was angry that Sigrid was abandoning *our* plans." Erik sighed. "We had a terrible quarrel. Sigrid married Braxton, and I came here."

"You've got a *sister?*" Johanna looked as if she was still getting used to the idea. "But why didn't you tell anyone?"

Erik scuffed the toe of one boot on the floor. "I was ashamed that I'd let a quarrel come between us," he confessed. "And my feelings were hurt, too. I just didn't want to talk about it."

"So that explains why you hid her photograph away," Kirsten said. "But why did you put the newspaper there, too?"

He looked even more embarrassed. "I didn't want people to know I was getting the newspaper. I folded my copy into my pocket that night at your place, hoping no one would notice." He spread his hands. "The subscription was a luxury I probably shouldn't have indulged in. But I believed my lumber would earn more than I needed to pay my debt. The newspaper is my only way to practice reading English and to learn about Minnesota. And it got mighty lonesome at that shanty without Sigrid to talk to."

Kirsten nodded slowly. When she imagined Erik all alone in his little shanty, it was hard to begrudge him a newspaper subscription.

"Kirsten," Johanna said, "you were so clever to figure out why the newspaper made Erik leave!"

"The only thing I *couldn't* figure out for sure were the two little parcels," Kirsten said.

"Especially the button. What was that about?"

"Braxton gave Sigrid a silk cape with pearl buttons before they got married," Erik explained. "I told her she was putting on airs, wearing such a fancy thing, but she loved it."

"The button is pretty," Kirsten admitted. "The cape must have been beautiful."

"Ja." Erik got up and began to pace. "But in time, Mr. Braxton proved himself to be an unkind husband. Sigrid tried writing to me, but he found the letter and tore it up. He was so furious that Sigrid didn't dare write another letter. She sent me the button instead, hoping I'd recognize it and come looking for her."

"So it *was* a sign!" Kirsten cried.

"Yes. Sigrid grew so miserable that she left her husband and moved in with a friend. But she was afraid that Mr. Braxton had talked with the man who carries the mail, and that he might have gotten the parcel containing the button, too. So she asked her friend to deliver the marble to Maryville. Sigrid didn't know Braxton had put that notice in the newspaper."

Erik smiled grimly. "But Braxton's last mean gesture—printing that notice threatening anyone who tried to help her—is what let me know that Sigrid needed me. I found her before he did."

"Where is Sigrid now?" Johanna asked anxiously.

"Safe at the shanty," Erik said.

"But why didn't you tell someone you were leaving?" Kirsten asked.

Erik stared out the window. "When I first read that notice, all I could think about was getting to Sigrid. After I started out, I did consider stopping here, or at your place." He nodded at Kirsten. "I just couldn't bring myself to do it. It was so very late! I didn't want to wake people up and take the time to explain everything." Erik's eyes were dark with regret. "But I'll admit I was also embarrassed about the whole situation."

More secrets! Kirsten thought. Everything would have been easier if Erik had told his friends about his sister from the beginning, and if Johanna and Mr. Green had told their friends about Mrs. Green's troubles.

"And I didn't realize that I'd be so delayed in Saint Paul!" Erik was saying. "It took me several days to work things out so that Sigrid could safely leave the city. I had to build a man a fence to earn enough money to pay the lawyer who helped us. Then Sigrid and I walked—"

"Erik!" Mr. Green exclaimed as he came through the front door, startling everyone. "Where have you been?"

"Where's Mama?" Johanna interrupted.

Mr. Green put a hand on her shoulder. "She's fine, child. She's going to spend the night with the Werners."

"Now that I'm back, I hope I can lift a little of the burden off your shoulders," Erik told him. "But I need to make things right with Olav first. Somehow. He lost his oxen on account of me."

Erik looked so bleak that Kirsten's heart twisted. "Maybe we can still get Starke and Fläckis back," she said, although she knew the chances were small.

Johanna turned to her father. "Papa, we've got a new problem with Mama." She explained what Kirsten had discovered in the *tine.*

"I'm sorry, Kirsten." Mr. Green raked his fingers through his hair. "My wife didn't mean any harm. I hope you believe that."

"Oh, I do," Kirsten said quickly. "And please, if there's anything Aunt Inger and Mama can do to help—oh!" Kirsten darted to the window and felt her heart slide toward her shoes when she saw how deep the shadows had grown. "I have to go!"

"I'll drive you," Mr. Green said. "It'll be quicker."

Erik held up a hand. "Why don't I drive Kirsten home? Then I can go looking for her papa and uncle. That way you can stay here with Johanna."

The men quickly had the black horse harnessed to the Greens' small wagon. After Kirsten hugged Johanna good-bye, Mr. Green put a hand on her arm. "I'm sorry for frightening you yesterday in the root cellar," he said quietly. "I'd gotten turned around in the woods, and I knew my wife would be frantic. I didn't mean to bark at you. I was just worried."

"It's all right," Kirsten told him.

He smiled gratefully. "I put a sack in the back of the wagon with some fresh venison in it for your family."

Kirsten thanked him and climbed to the wagon seat. Then she and Erik set off into the deep blue twilight.

Shadows left the road in gloom, and Kirsten couldn't help wondering what animals might be watching. "Tell me about your sister," she said, eager for distraction.

They were more than halfway home, with Erik in the middle of a story about learning to ski, when Svarten suddenly tossed his head and broke into a gallop. "Hold up there, boy," Erik called. "The road's too rough for that." The horse slowed to a walk but nickered, clearly unhappy.

"What's bothering him?" Kirsten asked, feeling a twinge of unease.

Erik glanced over his shoulder, and his expression changed. "I think we'll trot after all," he said, and clucked to Svarten. "There's a wolf following the wagon."

"A *wolf!*" Kirsten cried. There were no log walls to protect her here! "Is it coming after *us?*"

"The wolf probably just smelled the meat in the back of the wagon," Erik muttered. "But it's scaring Svarten."

Kirsten clenched the seat as the wagon picked up speed on the rough road. If the frightened horse bolted, the wagon could overturn or crash into a tree.

"Is the wolf still with us?" Erik asked.

Kirsten didn't think she could bear to see a wolf without even a pane of glass between them. "I can't look!"

"Yes, you can," Erik said evenly. "I need to watch the road."

Kirsten took several moments to steady her nerves, then forced herself to look back. Cold sweat slicked her skin. "Yes—it's trotting along behind us."

"Hang on," Erik muttered. Then he called, "Up, boy!" Svarten responded immediately. Kirsten clung to the seat with aching hands as the wagon bounced over rocks and ruts. *I mustn't fall off,* she thought desperately.

"Is it still following?" Erik asked. He had braced his feet wide against the front board, struggling to keep his balance and still maintain control of the frightened horse.

Kirsten felt tears sting her eyes. She dared another look over her shoulder and saw the wolf loping behind the wagon now, its tongue dangling from its open mouth. *"Ja!* Oh Erik, what are we going to do?"

"Is there anything in the wagon bed? Anything you can throw at it?"

Throw at it? That would involve letting go of the wagon seat, and Kirsten's hands felt frozen to the wood. "Just the venison," she said.

"Then I need you to climb back there and toss it out."

"Nej!" she cried. She was afraid to try climbing over the seat while the wagon jounced along.

And she absolutely could not face the wolf.

"I've got all I can handle to keep the horse under control," Erik said urgently. "I need your help, Kirsten. You can do it."

Kirsten wished she were safe in her cabin. She wished she were back in Sweden. She wanted to tell Erik that he was asking too much of her. But when she opened her mouth, what came out instead was a tiny "I'll try."

"Good." Erik kept his gaze on the road ahead, struggling to avoid the worst bangs and bumps as Svarten galloped through the twilight. He managed to hold the lines in one hand, and he clamped his other hand on Kirsten's wrist. "I've got you," he told her. "Go ahead and climb into the wagon bed."

Kirsten hesitated, gathering her courage. Then, half climbing and half falling, she scrambled over the seat. A wheel hit a rut, and her knees banged painfully against the floor of the wagon bed, but Erik's grip kept her from bouncing out. Kirsten found a good handhold and called, "I'm over."

"Now, see if you can pitch the deer meat out of the wagon."

Kirsten snaked her free hand into the burlap sack. Mr. Green had wrapped a haunch of venison in a piece of muslin. Kirsten tried to wrap her fingers around it but knew immediately that it was too heavy for her to lift. If she could have used both hands, if the wagon weren't crashing along at top speed, if fear weren't still making her muscles feel like cornmeal mush—but not now.

But the wolf still ran behind the wagon. How long would it be content to smell the meat before it jumped into the wagon to take it? That thought turned Kirsten's insides to ice.

"You can do it!" Erik called. "I know you can!"

I don't know that! Kirsten wanted to whimper. She scrabbled frantically in the sack again—and her fingers found a smaller package at the bottom, beneath the haunch. It was probably some choice cut that Mr. Green had intended to be a treat for her family.

Now her family wouldn't have even this rough gift. As she yanked the smaller package from the sack, Kirsten suddenly felt something new inside, a hot anger that boiled up and burned away her fear. For the first time, she stared hard at the wolf still tagging behind the wagon. "Here!" she yelled, and hurled the piece of meat as hard as she could. "Now *go away!*"

The wolf fell upon the venison and almost immediately faded into the evening as the black horse galloped on toward home.

"And *stay* away!" Kirsten shouted, although she could no longer even see the wolf. She kept yelling, determined now to scare away not just the wolf but the dark night itself, and her homesickness, and her grief, and every other beast that had stalked her since leaving Sweden. *"Just leave us alone!"*

12
Choices

"Good gracious!" Miss Mobeck exclaimed, leaning forward. "I would have been terrified of tumbling right out of the wagon!"

"I was," Kirsten admitted. "And I ended up covered with bruises! But we got home safely." Even now, almost two weeks after that frantic chase, she could hardly believe what had happened.

"You were very brave," the author told her.

"Erik helped me." Kirsten gave him a grateful look. "I couldn't have done it by myself."

Everyone had gathered at the Larson farm again: the Greens, the Vanstrums, the Bergs, Erik and Sigrid Sandahl, and Miss Mobeck and Reverend Trulsson, who had circled back after their trip to western settlements. They were picnicking in the barn this time, since rain showers were passing over the farm. Kirsten didn't mind. She liked inhaling the musty-sweet smell of grain and hay, liked hearing the raindrops drum on the roof, liked looking through the barn doors to watch the clouds burst.

"Erik is good at helping people," Sigrid murmured. Kirsten smiled at Erik's sister, who was as pretty as her photograph. She was shy, too—or perhaps just sad. Kirsten hoped that Sigrid's heart would mend. At least Sigrid had Erik, who was clearly delighted that she once again shared the dream of making a farm in Minnesota.

"So much has happened since I left!" Miss Mobeck said. "I guess my readers should know that life in Minnesota can be full of challenges." She looked from Erik to Uncle Olav. "I must say, I'm amazed you were able to get your oxen back."

Uncle Olav was sitting on the floor, leaning against a support post. "It took some doing," he assured her. "When the sheriff told us that Starke and Fläckis had already been sold, I thought they were gone for good. But Erik talked the sheriff into telling us who'd bought our team."

"I think the sheriff felt bad about the whole mess," Erik said.

"So the sheriff had already paid your debt with the money he got from selling Starke and Fläckis?" Miss Mobeck asked.

"Ja." Erik nodded. "With the money I had left over from that fence-building job, and a little that Olav had saved, we were able to rent a team of oxen. I used them to haul my lumber to town. There's a building boom going on in Saint Paul, and I got more money than I'd expected for my lumber—"

"So he could buy back *our* team!" Peter interrupted, a huge grin splitting his face.

"Right," Erik agreed. "I tracked down the man who'd bought Starke and Fläckis. He's a Norwegian immigrant. Nice fellow. Once I'd explained everything, he was willing to help me out. I used some of my lumber money to buy Starke and Fläckis back. Then the Norwegian used the money I gave him to buy another team."

"And you were able to get your harvest in," Reverend Trulsson said, looking at the huge pile of wheat bundles stacked in the barn.

"We did lose some," Uncle Olav said. "We were still working when a storm hit. But we saved most of it. We'll get by."

"Thanks to our neighbors," Papa said, looking around the circle.

Kirsten felt warm inside as she remembered how everyone had pitched in. The Berg brothers and Mr. Vanstrum had helped get the wheat into the barn. Mr. Green had let Erik keep the horse and wagon long enough to drive to Saint Paul so that he and Uncle Olav and Papa could talk with the sheriff.

"Here's something else your readers should think about," Papa told Miss Mobeck. "Back in Sweden, I lived my whole life in the same village. I knew everyone, and they knew me. Once

I came here, it was harder than I'd expected to trust people I didn't know. Even Swedes."

Me too, Kirsten thought. She hadn't liked watching Papa blame Erik for causing trouble, but when she'd seen her amber heart in Johanna's *tine,* she'd learned for herself how easy it was to assume the worst. Thank goodness she and Johanna had talked everything through! But thinking about her friend made a lump rise in Kirsten's throat. If only . . . Kirsten pressed her shoulder against Johanna, who was sitting beside her. Johanna pressed back, with a look that said, *I know just how you feel.*

Miss Mobeck might have noticed their exchange, for she turned to Johanna's parents. "And you've decided to go back to Sweden?"

"We have." Mr. Green nodded. "It was a hard choice, but this new country isn't right for everyone."

"I tried," Mrs. Green said simply. "I'll never be happy here, though."

"And I made mistakes." Mr. Green leaned back on his hands. "I'm a good fisherman and a fair hunter, but not a farmer. I should have invested in oxen, not a horse. I spent money on luxuries I couldn't well afford. I was trying to live like an American, and to make a good life for my wife and daughter, but . . ." He shrugged, a rueful expression on his face.

Kirsten leaned close to whisper in Johanna's ear. "We'll take very good care of Svarten, I promise!" Uncle Olav had made arrangements to buy the black horse—with money loaned by Erik. Uncle Olav had protested, but Erik had insisted. "It's the least I can do after all the trouble I caused," he'd said, and the deal had been made.

"Svarten will be happy here," Johanna told Kirsten. "And I'll be glad to know he's with you. Maybe you should start calling him by his English name, though. Papa says 'Svarten' means 'Blackie.'"

"Blackie," Kirsten repeated, trying out the strange new word. "I guess Blackie is my first truly American friend. But oh, Johanna, I wish you weren't going!" Kirsten felt as if all she'd been doing for months was saying good-bye to people she cared about. When she remembered how much she'd envied Johanna her horse, and her two windows, and her sugar cones wrapped in pretty blue paper, Kirsten's cheeks flushed hot with regret.

"I'm sad, but I'm glad too," Johanna said honestly. "Mama will be better when we go back to Sweden. Papa will be a fisherman again. I'll be with my cousins, and people won't call me a strange American name." She picked up a piece of straw and twirled it in her fingers. "We're giving up, but . . . well, it's for the best."

❤

When the rain let up a short while later, Johanna and her parents said their good-byes. Kirsten gave her friend a fierce hug. "Please write to me!" she begged.

"I will!" Johanna promised. "And we'll make sure your grandparents get the letters you wrote, too."

Kirsten stood in the muddy yard, watching until the Green family—no, the *Sjögren* family—disappeared into the woods. She didn't see Mama until she felt a hand squeeze her shoulder. "Your friendship with Johanna won't end just because she's back in Sweden," Mama said softly. "Every time you brush the black horse, you'll feel close to Johanna again."

Kirsten struggled to push words past the lump in her throat. "Do you think so?"

"I do." Mama patted the knitting needles sticking out from her pocket. "Just as knitting keeps me close to Mormor. She taught me to knit, many years ago."

Kirsten thought that over. So *that* was why Mama had done so much knitting lately! She'd been knitting away the distance between herself and Mormor. "Mama? Can we have another lesson tonight?"

Mama smiled. "I'd like that."

Papa walked across the yard to join them, his boots squelching through puddles. "So,

Kirsten," he said. "Do you wish we were headed back to Sweden like your friend?"

"Nej!" The word popped out, but Kirsten realized it was true. "Even when things were really hard, I never thought about giving up." She considered that, then added, "Not for long, anyway."

"We're making our home here," Mama agreed. "I wish I'd gotten to know Johanna's mother, though, instead of thinking about my own troubles. I won't make that mistake again."

"We're all learning as we go." Papa put his arm around his wife's shoulder. "From what Kirsten told us, Johanna's mother needed more than you would have been able to give her."

"Johanna's mother lost heart," Kirsten said sadly.

"I'm afraid so," Papa said. "But *you* never did. I'm proud of you, daughter."

"Kirsten!" It was Sigrid, calling from the barn door. "We're going to play marbles! Come join us!" For the first time, Sigrid looked more like a cheerful schoolgirl than an unhappy wife.

"I'll be right there!" Kirsten called. But she lingered a moment, standing between her parents, gazing around the farm. The earth smelled fresh, and the water dripping from eaves and leaves promised new growth.

The wolves can howl tonight, Kirsten thought. *The storms can come.* The Larson family would manage somehow. They were here to stay.

Looking Back

A Peek into the Past

This Swedish painting shows weeping relatives saying a last good-bye to departing immigrants.

In Kirsten's time, thousands of families from Sweden and other northern European countries sailed to America. Most were drawn by the hope of finding land of their own to farm. Like the Larsons, many of these immigrants headed straight for the prairies and woodlands of Minnesota, Wisconsin, Iowa, and the Dakotas.

There, the settlers found what they were seeking—good land that they could turn into farms. But the challenges that faced them were huge.

Many settlers started their new lives on the frontier in one-room, hand-built log cabins.

Most settlers made rough, cramped homes of logs or sod and did

Oxen were prized for farmwork because they are stronger and sturdier than horses.

the backbreaking work of clearing, plowing, and harvesting their land by hand. Because they put all their money into land and seed at first, families had to save for years before they could afford oxen to do the hardest labor.

Women often helped with field work and then went inside to face housework as well. One Minnesota settler wrote, "My husband used to go to bed tired to death and leave me sitting up working. Then he would find me up no matter how early it was. He said I never slept." A young boy recalled, "I can remember after many a long and hard day in the field, Mother would sit up half the night making our clothing, knitting, etc."

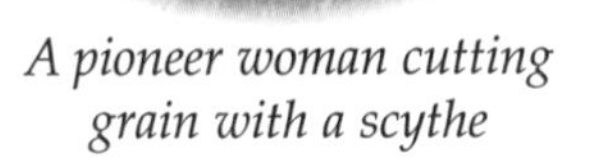

A pioneer woman cutting grain with a scythe

Mittens knitted in a traditional design

Milking cows was a daily chore for many girls.

Children worked hard, too. By age four, they helped with housework and farm chores. Children of nine or ten walked miles from home on errands and drove wagons alone.

Facing so much hardship, settlers relied on one another for help and friendship. Men worked on one another's farms to harvest crops, build fences, and raise barns. Women held work bees and simply offered one another comfort. One man recalled, "It was just a pleasure for ladies to take their knitting along and walk two or three miles to visit their neighbors and help them, too, if needed."

Guests—whether old friends, new neighbors, or strangers passing through—were

Quilting bees gave frontier women a chance to visit as they worked together.

welcomed and offered a place to stay, no matter how crowded a little cabin got.

Yet the frontier was always an uncertain place. Settlers knew that a single storm, an invasion of birds or insects, or a prairie fire could destroy the year's crops in a day. Bears, wildcats, rattlesnakes, and wolves were added dangers.

Wolves almost never harmed people, but many settlers talked about frightening experiences with them. "The timber wolves were plenty and fierce," one Minnesota settler wrote. "My sister was treed by a pack from nine o'clock until one. By that time we had got neighbors enough together to scatter them." From inside their homes, settlers often heard the wolves howling and saw them looking in their windows. Anyone traveling home after a hunting trip or after butchering at a neighbor's place risked having to give up the meat to hungry packs of wolves.

A Minnesota timber wolf

An Ojibwa mother holds her baby, wrapped in a cradleboard.

Many women and children were frightened by visits from Sioux and Ojibwa Indians, whose language and customs they did not understand. One Norwegian woman was so frightened by local Indians that her husband dug a hiding place in the ground and kept a candle and milk there. Whenever she saw unwanted guests approaching, she left tobacco or food on the table and hid in the hole.

Swedish writer Fredrika Bremer spent two years traveling in America in the 1840s. Her book, ***Homes in the New World,*** *told Swedes what to expect if they immigrated.*

Most settlers had some knowledge of their new home from letters written by those who had arrived earlier, just as Kirsten's family had letters from Uncle Olav. People considering immigrating might have read books or pamphlets by Swedish writers who had traveled to America to report on life in Swedish settlements, as the fictional Miss Mobeck does.

Precious keepsakes carried from Sweden were kept safe in hand-painted boxes.

Although immigrants usually settled near relatives and other people from their homeland, many struggled terribly with homesickness. Children learned not to ask their parents or grandparents about the old country, knowing it would make them cry. More than a few families gave up and returned to Sweden.

Yet despite the hardships, most immigrants stayed, believing they could give their children a better future in America. Today, the Midwest is dotted with farming communities that remember and celebrate the heritage of their immigrant ancestors—families very much like Kirsten's.

A Minnesota festival celebrates Swedish heritage.

Glossary of Swedish Words

Fläckis *(FLEH-kiss)*—Spot

god morgon *(gohd MOR-on)*—good morning

ja *(yah)*—yes

Johanna *(yoh-HA-na)*—a girl's name

kaffe *(KAH-feh)*—coffee

Kulla *(KUH-la, with the "uh" pronounced like the "u" in "pull")*—girl (in an old dialect of Swedish)

nej *(nay)*—no

Mormor *(MOR-mor)*—Grandma (used only for the mother's mother; the father's mother is called by a different name)

Sjögren *(SHEW-grehn)*—a Swedish last name

smörgås *(SMUWR-gahss)*—an open-faced sandwich

Starke *(STARK-eh)*—Strong One

Svarten *(SVAHR-ten)*—a horse's name

tack *(tahk)*—thank you

tine *(TEE-na)*—a wooden container

välkommen *(vehl-KO-mehn)*—welcome

Author's Note

Would you like to learn more about how it felt to immigrate to America as Kirsten did? You may wish to visit one of the museums dedicated to telling that story. You can explore the history of Swedish settlement in Minnesota at the American Swedish Institute in Minneapolis and at Gammelgården Museum in Scandia. Old World Wisconsin in Eagle, Wisconsin; the Swedish American Museum Center in Chicago, Illinois; and many other sites also provide glimpses into the lives of families who traveled from Europe to the United States in the nineteenth century.

To learn more about wolves, and to separate fact from tall tale about these sometimes-misunderstood animals, visit the International Wolf Center in Ely, Minnesota. You can also stop by their Web site, www.wolf.org.

I'm grateful for the many people and organizations, past and present, who preserved the stories and artifacts that helped me imagine life in an early Swedish American community. Thanks also go to the staff at the Minnesota History Center's Library and Archives for their research assistance, and to Eva Apelqvist for her help with Swedish names.

About the Author

The author at work as a museum guide

Kathleen Ernst is a writer and a historian. She spent twelve years working at a living-history museum called Old World Wisconsin, where she experienced firsthand what daily life in Kirsten's time was like.

She is now a full-time writer. Her many books for children and teens include *Secrets in the Hills: A Josefina Mystery* and two Kit mysteries, *Danger at the Zoo* and *Midnight in Lonesome Hollow.* She also wrote three American Girl History Mysteries: *Trouble at Fort La Pointe; Whistler in the Dark;* and *Betrayal at Cross Creek.*

Trouble at Fort La Pointe was an Edgar Award nominee for Best Children's Mystery. *Danger at the Zoo, Whistler in the Dark,* and *Betrayal at Cross Creek* were all nominated for the Agatha Award for Best Children's/Young Adult Mystery.